DEEP WATERS

Liz Marshall receives a letter from her father, asking her to cut short her holiday in Miami to fly to the remote Caribbean island of Grand Guani to find out why her brother, Nick, had left a promising career in the RAF to work for a small airline there. When she arrives, Nick greets her warmly and books her into the Guani Inn, next door to the quarters he shares with Tom Channing, an American diver. But why does Liz receive such a cold reception from Tom and everyone else she encounters? And why were Nick and Tom so keen for her to leave the island?

Books by Barbara Whitnell
Published by The House of Ulverscroft:

THE SONG OF THE RAINBIRD
THE RING OF BELLS
THE SALT RAKERS
LOVEDAY
THE CAROLINE QUEST
CHARMED CIRCLE
THE MILL COTTAGE
THE FRAGRANT HARBOUR

BARBARA WHITNELL

◆

DEEP WATERS

Complete and Unabridged

ULVERSCROFT
Leicester

First published in Great Britain in 1977
under the title 'Edge Of The Deep'
by Ann Hutton

First Large Print Edition
published 2001
by arrangement with
Severn House Publishers Limited
Surrey

British Library CIP Data

Whitnell, Barbara
    Deep waters.—Large print ed.—
    Ulverscroft large print series: general fiction
    1. West Indies—Fiction
    2. Suspense fiction
    3. Large type books
    I. Title
    823.9'14 [F]

    ISBN 0–7089–4482–5

Published by
F. A. Thorpe (Publishing)
Anstey, Leicestershire
Set by Words & Graphics Ltd.
Anstey, Leicestershire
Printed and bound in Great Britain by
T. J. International Ltd., Padstow, Cornwall

This book is printed on acid-free paper

1

I couldn't get away from Miami quickly enough. Everyone knows that it's people who make places, so I attach no blame to that — in parts — attractive metropolis. In fact, I had a pretty shrewd suspicion as the plane seemed to be pulsating on the end of the runway for ever and a day, that if there were any blame to be attached anywhere, it would come flying to me like a homing pigeon. Who but Liz Marshall, with her high IQ and her honours degree, could have made quite such a hash of the whole situation?

Thank heaven we were off at last and the geometrically placed, box-like houses (surely they had to be more attractive than they appeared from the air?) were falling away beneath us. Goodbye to the golf course and the marinas; the funny, flattened cars progressing silently along the freeway; the concrete jungle of luxury hotels that lined the beach. Here at last was the open sea, with nothing between me and the island but three hours of air space.

You can do a lot of thinking in three hours. Although I told myself it was a negative exercise, it was impossible not to think of Wayne Everett. I could imagine him going back to his car, having seen me off at the airport. I felt sure he would be smiling that downward-turned smile which meant he was inwardly pleased. Oh, he had gone through the motions; had promised to write, had politely regretted that I had to cut my holiday short. But he was no fool. He knew as well as I that the whole affair was over — finito, kaput. Deader than the proverbial dodo.

Where had it all gone wrong? He had seemed such a twin soul when we had met in London — he a visiting professor in English Literature, and I a teacher of the same. We seemed to have so much in common and I had looked forward to my visit to his country for the past six months. Where could all the fun and the laughter and shared interests have gone? There were times, those last few days, when I had looked at him in amazement; surely this was a stranger, this opinionated, overbearing young man? Or was it merely that Wayne Everett, on his best behaviour in a foreign capital, was a different proposition from Wayne Everett on his home territory?

Undoubtedly it had been a relief to leave; but underneath the relief I was conscious of sadness too, and an uncomfortable suspicion that it had all happened before — the attraction, the disillusionment, the headlong flight. There were times when I suspected that I was no more mature than the fourteen-year-olds I taught in school. Was I destined to take fright and run at the barest prospect of any serious involvement?

Oh well. There was nothing to be gained by rehashing the whole ghastly episode — and in any case, it is an ill wind that blows nobody good. If I hadn't been staying in Miami, my father would never have asked me to go to the island to find Nick. And I would not now be flying over impossibly turquoise-blue water and a chain of little islands, strung out like beads on a thread. I took out my father's letter once again, smiling to myself as I smoothed the pages. The tone of it was so typical — never for one moment had he considered that I might not be willing to cut my holiday short and fly off to the back of beyond to do his bidding. Had things been different, I would have been less amenable. Perhaps. Instant obedience was something that had been pretty well ingrained.

'Your brother has at last communicated with me,' he had written. 'I want you to drop everything and fly down to this god-forsaken island where he has chosen to bury himself, and do what you can to talk some sense into him. I gather there are two planes a week.'

Try to influence Nick? I had never been able to do that, nor did I think it any part of my duty to try. But it would be interesting to find out the reasons for his seemingly inexplicable behaviour, and above all, it would be wonderful to see him again. The rest of the family might regard him as a bit of a black sheep, but of my three brothers he had always been my favourite, closer to me than any of the others. I never felt that they had been genuinely concerned for his wellbeing during his silence of the last few months; they had taken the attitude that really, one might have expected it of Nick.

'How fortunate,' my father had gone on, 'that you are staying in Miami, comparatively near Grand Guani. (Did you know, by the way, that this is one of our last remaining colonies in the Caribbean? The encyclopædia gives it in two lines: it states it is chronically short of water and that hurricanes are not infrequent. What Nick can be thinking of I cannot imagine).

'Tell him I am prepared to forget past disappointments. If he comes home, I will do my best to pull strings to get him into a reputable airline. How he can have thrown away his career prospects with the RAF to fly with this tuppeny-hapenny airline is beyond my comprehension. I rely on you to shake some sense into the young puppy.'

I smiled again, but sadly this time. In the twenty-four years of Nick's life, my father seemed to have learned nothing about him or what made him tick. I knew that nothing would alienate Nick more than the assumption that he needed his father to pull strings — that he was unable to arrange his own life. If any of these messages were to be passed on, there would be a good deal of rephrasing for me to do.

But it *was* good to think of seeing him again! I hoped that he would be at the airport to meet me. I'd had no time for more than a telegram announcing my arrival and felt very much as if I was launching myself into the unknown.

What would it be like, this island that I had never heard of, that was accorded a scant two lines in the Encyclopædia Brittanica? It would surely be attractive for Nick to decide to live there? Palm trees and white beaches, and laughing, brown-skinned maidens, I imagined. On reflection, it did sound rather his scene.

The reality came as something of a shock. The island came rushing to meet us, rocky and treeless and covered in a low, sparse scrub. There were patches of green foliage, but the overall impression was drab, as if a layer of dust covered the island from end to end.

Somehow I had not imagined it to be so small. From the air it was possible to see it in its entirety — a brown smudge surrounded by a smooth blue sea, gentle waves creaming against the shore. As we landed, I could see that it was shabby. To the left of the runway was an expanse of inland water, shallow and polluted, with the skeleton of a windmill leaning drunkenly to one side, and as we turned towards the airport buildings (if they could be dignified by such a name) I saw that they were utilitarian in the extreme, either still being built or in the process of falling down. It was hard to see which. But there — and how thankful I was — I could see Nick.

He looked different. Well, I told myself, of course he's bound to — wasn't he in RAF uniform the last time I'd seen him? Lots of spit and polish and a regulation haircut. Now he was dressed in white shorts and an open-necked shirt, a pilot's stripes on his epaulettes. His dark hair fell to well below his ears and he was deeply tanned, but when I eventually saw him coming towards me as I came down the steps from the plane, I knew that he had changed very little. He still had that same slouch, deplored by my father, and the same smile.

He stood off a little and looked at me, grinning crookedly in the same old way.

'Well, now,' he said. 'If it isn't Liz!'

'Nicholas Marshall, as I live and breathe!'

We laughed and hugged each other.

'Oh Nick, it's so lovely to see you,' I said.

'Great to see you, too. You're looking marvellous.' He studied me carefully, holding me by the shoulders. 'Hey, you've had your hair cut.'

'And you haven't!'

'And I bet you're thinking how Dad would disapprove. Which, I imagine, brings us rather neatly to the purpose of your visit.'

'For heaven's sake let my feet touch the ground before you start bristling at me. We can talk later.'

It was considerably later as things turned out. Customs and immigration formalities were conducted in a leisurely manner. Why hurry? It was far too hot. But eventually we were driving away from the airport in an incredibly dilapidated American car which would have done justice to any scrap heap in the world.

'Don't drop anything,' Nick warned me. 'It goes straight through to the road.'

'How does it keep going?'

7

'You'll find ninety percent of the cars on the island are like this. It's the salt air — everything rusts ten times as quickly as anywhere else. But it gets me around. It's not as if one has to drive long distances.'

The road was bordered on each side by a sandy waste. There were a few garden-less, concrete block houses set down apparently at random among the thorn bushes, but apart from two donkeys who stared at us incuriously from the side of the road and a posse of raggle-taggle dogs, there was no sign of life.

I was bewildered. Nothing I saw made sense of Nick's decision to leave the RAF and Washington.

'Is it all like this?' I asked curiously.

He knew what I was thinking.

'It doesn't make what you'd call an immediate appeal, does it?' He smiled down at me. 'But you'll find that the little town has a certain charm and the beaches are out of this world. You know,' he went on, 'it really *is* good to see you. But don't think I don't know why you're here. Dad's sent you hot foot in pursuit of the prodigal son.'

'Yes, well . . . ' I knew it was useless to deny it. 'I'm only committed to passing on all sorts of messages and finding out how you are. I haven't promised anything else. It was worrying, not hearing from you for so long.'

Nick bit his lip. 'I know — I feel bad about that. But the more I *didn't* write, the harder it was to get started.' He drove for a bit in silence. 'I hope you're not going to nag me about leaving here. You'd be wasting your time.'

'Nick, your life is your own affair. But I couldn't pass up the offer of a free trip to see you, could I?'

'What were you doing in Florida, anyway?'

'Staying with friends.' I'd decided to keep my own counsel about the disastrous Wayne affair — besides, I was distracted by the incredibly unattractive scenery which lay outside the car.

'I refuse utterly to believe this is a Caribbean island! We must have landed on the moon. What on earth does anyone *do* here?'

'Unfortunately, very little. Unemployment is a problem.'

'I can imagine. What are *you* doing, Nick?'

'Flying. You know that.'

'But why here?'

'I like it, strange as it may seem.'

'But how can you — oh, *that's* better!' We had rounded a corner and were now driving along a narrow road which skirted the sea. On our left was a dazzling beach, fringed with casuarina trees and beyond that the ocean, a translucent turquoise in the shallows, deepening to a sapphire blue further from the shore.

'Now that's a bit more like my idea of a Caribbean island.'

'I told you it had charm. First impressions aren't always the right ones, you know.'

'None better,' I said, with feeling. 'Is this where you live?'

Nick had brought his ramshackle car to a halt outside a large white wooden house set back from the road a little and facing the beach. It was half hidden behind a stone wall which spilled over with crimson bougainvillea.

'My dear girl, this is one of the most impressive edifices in the old part of town — the Guani Inn. Our quarters are on a more modest scale, right next door. No room for visitors, I'm afraid, so much as we should like to have put you up, I've had to book you into the pub.'

'Who's we?' I asked.

'Tom Channing and I. He's an American — a diver. A really great guy; I know you'll like him. You don't mind being farmed out at the hotel, do you?'

'Of course not. It looks rather nice.' I was already half out of the car. 'This Tom — is he responsible for your coming here?'

'No, I met him after I arrived. He was looking for someone to share expenses and we hit it off OK., so decided to team up. I heard about the job in Washington.'

'And it was irresistible, I suppose?' I asked dryly.

'Absolutely.' Nick was giving nothing away. 'Let's get inside before we're cooked to a frazzle.'

The Guani Inn was a typical old West Indian house, built of wooden planks almost two feet in width. The shutters, necessary in case of hurricanes, were painted green and so was the balcony which ran across the front of the house and had two outside staircases, one at each end of the building. The roof was of shingle, steeply pitched with three dormer windows, and I found it enchanting.

'It's well over a hundred years old,' Nick said, 'though there are modern extensions at the back. Would you mind fastening the gate? Otherwise the donkeys wander in and eat all Betty's cherished plants. I'm sure you'll be comfortable here. It isn't exactly the Ritz, but I asked them to give you a room overlooking the sea, and the food is quite good. It'll cost a bomb — everything does on this island — but I imagine Dad is footing the bill, isn't he? Ah, here's Betty.'

A faded blonde woman stood at the door

11

to meet us, and Nick introduced her as Betty Schroeder who, together with her husband Lew, owned and managed the hotel. She was small and neatly made, rather dashingly dressed in scarlet shorts and a halter top, but her face was haggard and her eyes strained behind her spectacles. Even though she smiled at us, she looked harassed as if her mind was elsewhere.

'I've given you a front room, as your brother asked.' Her voice was flat and nasal, but I was not sufficiently well versed in American accents to pin-point it geographically. 'He said you'd like the view, and I'm sure you will, the sea is such a beautiful colour, don't you think so? But some folks say it keeps them awake, the noise of the waves and all. It sure takes some getting used to.'

I opened my mouth to reply, but closed it again as she rattled on.

'I sure hope the maids cleaned the room good. I told them to, but you know how it is, nothing's done properly unless you see to it yourself. The islanders would sleep all day if you let them.'

She had been leading us up a central staircase and now unlocked a door at the top of the stairs, revealing a single room that had obviously been part of a much larger one at some time. It was adequately, if not luxuriously furnished, and seemed perfectly clean to me.

Betty tested the fan in the corner, which failed to work. Her brow creased in annoyance.

'Gee, this was working yesterday — I'll have to get Truman to fix it. Still and all, you probably won't need it. There's always a good breeze from the sea, after sundown. Say, will you be in for dinner?'

I looked enquiringly at Nick.

'Will I?'

'Yes, I think so. Will you book us a table for three, Betty? Tom will be eating with us.'

'Sure thing. Well, I'll leave you to get settled in. Guess you have a lot to talk about.'

'She doesn't do too badly herself, does she?' I commented, after the door had closed behind her. I went over to the open glass door which led on to the balcony.

'Oh Nick, this is lovely.'

'Good thing you haven't a penchant for swinging cats,' Nick said, withdrawing his head from the tiny shower room. 'That's about two feet square.'

'I couldn't care less,' I said. 'Look at the view!'

I stepped outside and the heat hit me like a blow.

'Is it always as hot as this?'

'At this time of the year. If you will come in August! Look Liz, why don't I push off now and let you have a shower or whatever, and you come over to the cottage as soon as you like. You know where it is, don't you? The very next gate to the left of the hotel. I'll have an ice-cold beer at the ready.'

'Sounds blissful!'

It was barely half an hour later when, showered and changed into brief shorts and a thin blouse tied above my midriff, I found my way to the cottage. Nick had not exaggerated when he described it as hardly big enough for two, in fact I don't think I have ever seen a smaller house. It was only the width of one room across and that did duty as a combined kitchen, living and dining room.

Yet it was attractive. The kitchen, with its sink, stove and fridge, was half-hidden behind a formica topped counter at one side of the room at the far end, and here too was a round dining table and four chairs. The main part of the room was taken up by four low, white chairs with orange cushions that were grouped round a circular sisal rug. A beautifully marked rectangular piece of wood, polished to within an inch of its life and supported by stone blocks, served as a coffee table, and more planks separated by similar blocks were set one on top of the other against the wall, making a set of shelves on which were books and records and a sophisticated hi-fi system.

'That's ingenious,' I remarked, looking at the shelves as Nick went to the fridge for a beer. 'You've really made yourself comfortable. Whose idea was that?'

'Tom's. He had the whole place fixed up by the time I joined him.'

'He must have quite a flair. That's nice too.' I indicated a fishing net draped against one wall and hung about with glass floats. 'And what a lot of super books!'

Irresistibly drawn, I wandered over and read the titles with some amazement.

'Hey, if these are yours, someone's been educating you!' I said. 'Is Tom responsible for that, too? I never knew you to read anything more taxing than Harold Robbins.'

Nick made as if to throw the bottle at me.

'Don't be so bloody patronizing! But yes, most of them are Tom's — and he *is* educating me. He's quite a guy.'

'What's he like?'

Nick laughed.

'You'll have to meet him — there's no way I can describe him. He's thirtyish; quiet; very relaxed; very tough.'

'I can hardly wait.'

I was still on my feet, making a tour of the

15

room. An oil painting in a simple frame caught my attention and I stopped in front of it. It showed two boats drawn up under a group of casuarina trees with the beach stretching away beyond them to the sea. A crumbled sea wall was in the background, with a figure leaning idly against it. It was bold and simple, and somehow managed to convey a feeling of heat and indolence.

'I like that. Oh, I like that very much,' I said. 'It's the beach outside, isn't it? Who painted it Nick? Is it a local artist?' I peered at it closer to decipher the initials. 'Who's NM?' The significance suddenly struck me and I did a double take. 'NM! Not you, Nick?'

'Why not?' Nick smiled at me from one of the orange chairs where he had stretched himself. 'Come and sit down and stop pacing like a caged lion.'

I sat down opposite him, looking at him as if I'd never seen him before.

'Since when did you paint? What a dark horse you've turned out to be! Hey — ' a thought suddenly struck me. 'You're not doing a Gauguin on us, are you? Is that why you've come here?'

Nick laughed.

'The Moon and Two-and-a-half New Pence? Come off it, Liz, it isn't that good!

16

I've been painting for a hobby for quite a while now. A girl I met in Washington put me on to it. But it's purely for enjoyment — I don't kid myself there's any great merit in it.'

'I think that one's terrific.'

I studied him frowningly.

'You have changed, you know. I thought perhaps not, at first — but there's something . . . it's a bit difficult to put a finger on it.'

'Maybe I've just grown up.'

'Maybe.'

I paused before speaking again. I knew it wouldn't be easy, but wanted so much to understand.

'Nick, why did you come to this place?'

He sighed.

'I suppose we might just as well talk about it sooner as later, but I don't imagine I can ever make you understand. I guess you could say I was doing my own thing.'

'But the RAF was your own thing.'

He looked at me, an opaque expression in his hazel eyes, and I sighed. I knew that look of old. It meant he wasn't talking.

It was the self-same look that he used to turn on Father during a lecture on a bad school report or when asked for an explanation of some childish scrape; the look which used to drive our exasperated parent to demand of heaven why this youngest son

17

could not be more like his brothers.

Our mother had died when Nick was born and sometimes I felt that from that moment on, nothing he did was right. I was two years older than Nick. Nigel and James were almost grown up while we were children, or so it had seemed to us. They had covered themselves with glory at school, both in the classroom and on the playing field, but Nick was a different kettle of fish altogether. He was a rebel and it was not until he suddenly decided on the RAF as a career that he really got down to work. I shall never forget the night he woke me at some hour long past midnight to tell me how he had met this marvellous chap who'd taken him up in a plane and let him take the controls, and how the marvellous chap had said he'd never come across anyone with a more natural feel for flying, and how it had to be the RAF. It was almost as if he'd seen a vision, or been converted.

To everyone's astonishment, he did very well indeed, passing out of Cranwell almost at the head of his year. He trained and flew and was promoted; he came home on leave and talked to me for hours about his flying and his future, and altogether gave the impression of being ecstatically happy. Even Father was happy when he was sent to Washington as assistant to the assistant Air Attaché, and he was able to boast to his cronies at the Club about 'My Boy at the Embassy' as well as 'My Boy the Barrister' and 'My Boy in the City'. Most of them I knew well, were unaware of the existence of a third son, who extracted great amusement from the situation, making me swear never to explain to Father how very junior the assistant to the assistant Air Attaché was. I suppose it was hardly to be wondered at that Father was bitterly disappointed when he heard his wayward son had thrown the whole thing up to take a pilot's job in a tin-pot airline on a remote island.

Personally, I was mystified. And in spite of his mulish look, I pressed on.

'I'd like to understand, Nick.'

'You never will.'

'You could try me.'

He paused for a moment as if choosing his words carefully.

'You know I've always loved flying. Pushing bits of paper around in Washington wasn't my idea of fun.'

'But that was only temporary. You were on the way up!'

'Have you any idea what small fry I was?'

'Of *course* you were! What do you expect at the age of twenty four? Surely it was something to be out of the usual rut?'

'I felt like a battery hen! Look Liz, you've done your bit. Don't get involved with the whys and wherefores. You may think I'm an irresponsible idiot — and I'm damned sure the rest of the family do — but I'm a big boy now. I have to make my own decisions, for good or ill. So lay off — OK?'

'I don't mean to nag . . . but it *is* hard to understand. You were so passionately keen on the RAF — not just the flying, but the whole bit. Being part of the tradition. Doesn't it mean a thing to you any more?'

The obstinate, closed-in expression was even more pronounced, and when he spoke his voice was harsh.

'I said lay-off, Liz. I meant it.'

There was a small silence between us.

'Anything you say,' I said at last. 'Aren't you going to ask about the family?'

'Sure. How is the old man? And the wonder boys?'

'Dad's fine. Just as fiery, I suppose, but we all stand up to him a little more these days, and it's surprising how well he takes it.'

'We should have tried it years ago. I suppose he was pretty shaken by my — defection?'

'What do you think? He was sure you must have been caught cheating at cards in the mess, or got the Ambassador's daughter in the family way, or something.'

'Chance would have been a fine thing. She was quite a dish.' He sighed a little. 'No Liz, I left — as they say — of my own accord.'

'If you did want to go back to England,' I said, rather diffidently, 'I daresay Dad could be helpful in getting a job. He still has his contacts.'

Nick laughed.

'Did he say that? The modern-day equivalent of the fatted calf, I suppose. Poor Dad — I never did come up to scratch, did I? I wonder if he ever knew how I hated disappointing him. I would have loved to win cups and have my name on rolls of honour, like the others.'

'How could he have known? You went to great lengths to show how little you cared.'

'Never mind.' There was more than a touch of acid in his voice. 'Nigel and James more than made up.'

'Sibling rivalry? It's time you lost that chip on your shoulder, Nick. You'd like them if you knew them now.'

'Possibly. Well, never mind them. How are you?'

'Oh, me!' I shrugged. 'All right. In a rut, I suppose.'

'How's the job?'

'So-so. We have a new headmistress who's — difficult.'

'No man on the horizon?'

'Nobody special.' I didn't want to pursue that one, and felt a change of subject was in order. 'Tell me about Grand Guani, Nick. Why is it British?'

'Because once it produced salt and was quite a wealthy, profitable sort of place. A jewel in the Empire's crown. But the bottom fell out of the salt market — at least, salt produced in this non-mechanized sort of way — and Britain's stuck with it.'

'What do people do?'

'Very little. There's no agriculture, since nothing much grows here, and no industry. There's a little lobster fishing and a small amount of tourism. Britain pumps in aid. It's not nearly enough, but I daresay it's all she can afford — it seems to keep the island afloat, and that's all. It's been discovered recently by Americans and Canadians who want an unspoilt place in the sun to live, and of course that's given employment to builders and contractors. There are some quite impressive houses up on the north ridge. Otherwise — well, I don't know. People seem to scratch a living, and although there's a great deal of poverty, there doesn't seem to be any real malnutrition.'

'And this airline you work for — is it the one I flew in with?'

'Good Lord, no! That's in the big time compared with our little operation. We just fly internally round the Guani group of islands — North Guani, West Guani, Lion Cay, Tree Cay and back again. Just a domestic service.'

'And you enjoy it?' I know I sounded incredulous.

'Would I be here if I didn't?' He got up to get himself another beer and spoke with his back to me. 'By the way Liz, how long do you intend to stay?'

'I hadn't really thought. About a week, I suppose, more or less — I have to be back in London by the first week in September. Does it matter at this stage?'

'Well, not really.' He came back and sat down again, his eyes firmly fixed on the drink in his hand. 'It's just that I'm flying every day and you'll be on your own. I don't imagine it will be much fun for you.'

'Oh, don't worry about me. I shall be perfectly happy on the beach.'

'For a day or two, perhaps, but this isn't the tourist season. It's too damned hot for lying around on beaches. You'll be bored to tears in no time.'

'I don't bore easily. Besides, I'd see you in the evenings, wouldn't I? You can't be flying

23

all the hours there are.'

'Of course not — but honestly, Liz, there's damn-all to do here. You'll have had quite enough of it by the time the next plane goes.'

I looked at him unbelievingly.

'Nicholas Marshall, do I read you correctly? You wouldn't be trying to get rid of me by any chance?'

He laughed uneasily.

'Why on earth should I want to do that?'

'I don't know, Nick. Why would you?'

He was saved the necessity of replying by the arrival of Tom Channing, but though I was curious to meet this paragon of whom Nick appeared to think so highly, his somewhat overpowering presence did little to ease the tension that had suddenly sprung up between us.

There was, I thought, an awful lot of Tom Channing. He was above average height and broad to match, and as he was dressed in nothing but a pair of sawn-off jeans, the expanse of suntanned flesh thus exposed was considerable. Not that I am in the least prudish about the male form — far from it; there was nothing, that I could see, to stop Tom from making it all the way to the centrefold in 'Playgirl', and the best of luck to him. But the effect in the confined space of the cottage was devastating.

His light brown hair, sun-streaked, curled on his neck. A moustache followed the curve of his lip, and he smiled at me to reveal advertisement-white teeth. But his deep-set grey eyes were cold and watchful and his polite words of welcome seemed to me a mere formality. Instinctively I felt wary of him.

Relaxed, Nick had said. I knew what he meant. There was a kind of boneless strength about him that was apparent in the way he moved across the room to help himself to a beer from the fridge. Economy of movement is, I think, the term to use. He returned and collapsed into the chair next to mine.

'Any sign of the spares?' he asked Nick.

'No, nothing. Maybe on the next plane.'

'Sure — the story of my life! There's no way I can keep the boat running without them.'

'Lucky it's the slack season,' Nick said.

Tom laughed quietly.

'When isn't it?'

'What sort of people come here on holiday?' I asked. 'One never sees it advertised in holiday brochures.'

'It's for the discriminating,' Tom said. 'Non-conformists. People who want something different — simple and uncommercialized without tourist traps and gift shops. We have the best waters in the world for skin-diving, and the cleanest, most deserted beaches.'

'Really?' I said, and even to myself sounded stuffy and slightly patronizing. I didn't mean it that way. It was simply that there was something about Tom that made me curiously shy. But his eyes flickered to meet mine and I knew that it was the patronage he had noted, not the shyness. He looked at me with a certain grim amusement.

'Sure seems a shame you had to interrupt your holiday at Miami Beach,' he said, and I knew only too well that I had been marked down as the sort of girl who liked luxury hotels and gold-plated Cadillacs, despising what he considered the more worth-while, simple pleasures.

'I wanted to come,' I said lamely.

'Sure,' he agreed. For a moment I thought he was going to say more, but he lapsed into silence, allowing Nick to continue cataloguing the island's charms. But I was very aware of him sitting there in an inexplicably inimicable, passive sort of way, and began to feel sorry that he was to make a third at the dinner table. I knew that his presence would inhibit me.

Later, back at the hotel as I changed for dinner, I tried to talk myself out of this vague feeling of uneasiness. I must have imagined it,

I told myself — both Nick's wish to be rid of me and Tom's latent hosility. Nick had *said* it was good to see me, hadn't he? As for Tom, there was no reason except for my own silly shyness why he should be unfriendly.

I resolved to stop being so ultra-sensitive and concentrated on getting dressed. I chose a cool green and white halter-necked dress that I had bought with Wayne and Miami in mind — one that was already a favourite. At least, I thought, that's something I salvaged out of the wreck. One dress, evening, green and white, dining-by-candlelight for the use of. I knew I looked good in it.

I gave a last look in the mirror, turning to look at my back-view. How alike Nick and I are, I thought, seeing myself at this less familiar angle. The same pointed chin and short upper lip. The same dark hair and hazel eyes, too, though in that dress and with a judicious use of eye-shadow, my eyes looked distinctly green that night. You're all *right*, I told myself impatiently. There is *no need* to be shy with that large and overpowering American. With a last look, I went down to meet them.

The patio at the back of the old hotel had been extended to form a dining room with the bar at the far end of it. Dozens of potted plants and shrubs made it appear almost as if we were in a garden, though the patio was roofed and screened against mosquitoes. A small breeze had sprung up as night fell, and, clad as I was in my low-backed dress, I felt pleasantly cool for the first time since landing on Grand Guani.

Tom and Nick were propping up the bar when I joined them. Tom, in cream coloured slacks and a brown shirt, seemed slightly less formidable and greeted me politely, while Nick whistled appreciatively. See? I said to myself. Where's all the hostility now? You imagined the whole thing.

Lew Schroeder was officiating behind the bar and was almost too overwhelming in his efforts to be friendly. He was a short, plump man, with a trick of peering into the face of whoever he was talking to, as if confiding something to that person alone. Dinner, he told us apologetically, was going to be late. Details were given — quite meaningless to me — about Jimmy letting them down again and Betty having to be in the bar when she should have been in the kitchen, as Lew himself was clearing crates of liquor through customs; but no one except a visiting American family, scarlet with sunburn, seemed much dismayed. The guests gathered, but seemed happy enough to order drinks and wait patiently for the food to be ready.

28

Nick and Tom seemed to know everyone and introduced me to a number of people whose names, I was uncomfortably aware, I failed to register.

'I wish I were more like you Americans,' I said to a charming grey-haired lady at my side. 'How do you manage it? Remembering names, I mean.'

'It's a trick,' she told me. 'Did you notice I repeated your name? When Nick said 'This is my sister, Liz', I said 'Hallo, Liz'. Now it's imprinted on my memory.'

'It's a wonderful theory,' I said doubtfully, feeling quite sure it would never work for me. 'I must try it.'

'Well, until you do,' she said, let's start over. I'm Ellen — Ellen Myers. And over there is my husband, George. I'm willing to bet he's talking aeroplanes to Nick. He's thinking of buying his own.'

I blinked at the casualness of this statement. Ellen made it sound as if he was contemplating going to the store for a loaf of bread.

'How nice,' I said faintly.

'He travels such a lot. It would be a great convenience.'

'Are you down here on business?'

'Yes, we are. George has an interest in various hotels in this part of the world. We're trying to get one off the ground here, but the difficulties seem to be endless — we've been coming here off and on for the last eighteen months and still seem no nearer getting things settled.'

'How frustrating for you.'

'Frustrating for George, maybe, but I'm happy to come and stay here just as often as he likes. I'm a bit of a beachcomber at heart. I'm sure Nick must be pleased to see you,' she added, going off at a tangent.

'It's just wonderful to see him again,' I said, feeling that I was at least on sure ground there.

'He's just the nicest guy. We've flown a great number of miles with him. George thinks the world of him.'

I smiled at her happily.

'That's nice.'

'And Tom, too,' Ellen went on. 'They really are a great pair.'

You see? I said to myself. Everyone likes Tom. You're just being contrary. I looked over to where he was in deep conversation with two earnest gentlemen who had been pointed out to me as representatives from the Foreign and Commonwealth Office. They seemed to be listening with respectful attention to all he had to say.

Nick and George Myers turned to join us.

'Have you booked Nick for the Haiti trip?' Ellen asked her husband. 'You know I don't like to fly with anyone else.'

'You're much too flattering,' Nick smiled down at her. 'When did you want to go? I'm on scheduled flights all this week, but I think I'll be free for a charter at the weekend — maybe Saturday.'

'SHED — uled!' Ellen spoke the word lingeringly. 'I just love the way you English say that. Would it sound affected if I adopted it?'

George gave her a fond look.

'Impossibly so! There's no particular hurry about the flight, Nick. Any time during the next ten days will suit me, and I only want to be away for one night.'

'I'll check with the office and let you know.'

'I'd appreciate it. Here's your boss now.'

Nick turned to greet a couple who were approaching and introduced them as Phil and Stella Prophet, both English. Phil was a slight, non-descript man, whom I felt I would have to see more than once before recognizing him again; but Stella could hardly have been more of a contrast. She was a dark, flamboyant woman, attractive in a gypsyish sort of way, who talked incessantly with much vivacity and movement. She tossed her glossy head, rounded her eyes, shrugged her shoulders; showing off, the girls in my form would have called it, with Nick, it soon became apparent, as the principal target.

I was amazed, both at the obviousness of Stella's line and the way in which Nick went along with it. There were whispered asides, hand-cupping as he lit her cigarette, clutchings of arm as she rocked with laughter at one of his jokes. Certainly it was Stella who was making all the running, but from where I was standing, it didn't seem to me that Nick was at all averse to her attentions. I found it incomprehensible; it was certainly a fact that Nick had always appreciated a pretty girl, but Stella was no girl. She had to be at least ten years older than Nick, quite apart from the fact that she was a married woman with her husband looking on at all this by-play. And on top of that, she was, quite simply, not Nick's type. Or at least, not the type I had ever seen him take an interest in before. Could he possibly have changed so much?

A final burst of activity in the dining room heralded the arrival of dinner, and Betty Schroeder, arriving flushed from the kitchen, besought us all to take our places. The table for three was rapidly made into a table for five to accommodate the Prophets, which I found disappointing. I would much have preferred the company of Ellen and George, whom I found very agreeable.

Stella took good care that she was seated next to Nick, while I sat opposite with Tom. Phil was a silent presence at the end of the table. He seemed resigned to being totally ignored by everyone and I felt sorry for him and did my best to engage him in conversation — but either his mind was on his wife or he was no conversationalist. Each subject raised died still-born. I was grateful when Tom came to my rescue and talked about fishing, upon which subject Phil became positively loquacious, until Stella silenced him effectively by the simple expedient of telling him that he was boring everyone. He lapsed once more into silence and addressed himself to his lobster a la Créole.

The Myers were sharing a table with the Schroeders. It was that sort of a hotel — really more of a guest house, with the accent on an informal, family atmosphere; but I couldn't help thinking that Betty was the last person to make guests feel relaxed. Even from a distance of twenty yards it was clear that she was on edge. She gave the impression of being poised to scurry off on a sudden errand, peering this way and that in a worried manner through her tip-tilted spectacles as if constantly thinking of some task

33

left undone. The three young waitresses seemed perfectly competent, but Betty was unable to leave them alone. She persistently beckoned them or caught them by the apron as they passed her table, hissing instructions and admonitions until the poor girls looked completely bewildered.

I was particularly struck by the girl who was serving at our table. The fresh, gingham uniforms they all wore seemed to suit her more than the others, though perhaps it was merely that she was prettier and had a superb figure. Her skin was a gloriously golden coffee colour and her features neatly formed and doll-like.

'What race is she?' I asked as she left us. She looked quite different from the others who appeared purely negroid.

'She's Guanian,' Nick said. 'But prettier than most. They come in all colours. Originally they were negro slaves, brought here by the salt barons, but there's been a great deal of monkey business since those days. There are only a handful of surnames among the lot of them.'

'Oh, *super*!' cried Stella, clapping her hands delightedly.

I thought at first she was applauding the islanders fecundity, but soon realized that her gaze was directed elsewhere.

'Good old Jimmy — I was *hoping* you'd come.' All heads turned to see what was causing such excitement. 'Come and play for us this *instant!*'

A thin, delicately made young man with long blond hair and a beard, dressed in faded jeans and a shapeless T-shirt which urged all and sundry to make love, not war, had wandered on to the patio and stood blinking in the light as if wondering how he came to be there. He had, I thought, a smile of extraordinary sweetness, but it soon became obvious that Lew, for one, was not disarmed by it.

'Where the hell have you been?' he demanded angrily, with none of the ingratiating charm he had shown to his guests. 'You were supposed to be tending bar from six.'

'Sorry, boss,' the young man said in a voice which I instantly recognized as pure London. 'I got delayed.' But he continued to smile, seemingly impervious to the rebuke. 'Anyway, I'm here now, with the old guitar at the ready. Anyone want a tune?'

He wandered closer to our table where Stella was waving madly to attract his attention.

' 'The Streets of London' — oh, *do* play 'Streets of London', Jimmy.'

'Anything for you, love,' he said, but he

spoke absently, looking in my direction. 'Hallo!' He spoke to me, momentarily ignoring the others. 'We haven't met, have we? I'm Jimmy.'

'How do you do. I'm Liz — Nick's sister.'

'Nick's sister, eh? Nice to meet you.' With complete self-possession and totally unaware of Lew going purple with rage in the background, he drew up a chair next to me. 'It's good to see a new face on the island.'

'*Jimmy*,' wailed Stella from across the table. 'Come on! We've been waiting for you.'

He pulled a face in her direction. 'No peace for the wicked, I suppose. Got a fag for after, love?'

Stella handed him her cigarette case and he took one, putting it behind his ear. He got to his feet and picking up his guitar, ambled over to the bar and hitched himself on to a stool. He played a few random chords and then drifted into 'Streets of London' as requested by Stella, who squealed appreciatively.

We had arrived at the coffee stage, and it was pleasant to sit back and listen to him.

His voice was light and appealing. No Caruso was he, but the very imperfection of his voice lent a definite charm to the wistful pathos of the song. I listened to him with enjoyment and spontaneously turned to Tom on my right hand when he had finished and was acknowledging the scattered applause.

'He's good!' I said, with some surprise.

'I guess he has a small talent,' Tom drawled, after a moment.

'That sounds a bit grudging.'

'Does it? Maybe I'm prejudiced. I just don't like the guy.'

'That hardly affects the quality of his music. What's the matter with him?'

Tom was silent for a moment, concentrating on stirring his coffee.

'Plenty,' he said flatly.

I let it go, irritated by his air of superior knowledge and feeling certain that whatever he felt about Jimmy went double for me. The vibrations between us could hardly have been worse. In any case, there was no opportunity to continue the discussion as Jimmy had begun another song — 'Early Morning Rain.'

'I like him,' I said, rather defiantly I felt, when he had finished. 'He's good, whatever you say.'

Tom laughed shortly.

'Don't be taken in by that boyish charm, lady. That guy is out for one person only — himself. He hasn't even registered the fact that he let Betty down before dinner. A smile, a song, and the world's at his feet again — all sins forgiven.'

'Maybe he had a good reason.'

'Oh sure!' Tom's voice was mocking. 'Like falling asleep, or screwing a girl on the beach. He is one no-good bum.'

Why his condemnation of Jimmy should have nettled me so much, I can't quite explain. To me it had become almost a personal issue; his censorious attitude to the singer made my hackles rise, as if in his disapproval I could sense a similar lack of sympathy towards myself. I turned a remote profile to Tom and listened to Jimmy's next song, which was a calypso with a rather naughty chorus that had everyone stomping and clapping and joining in with high good humour. Everyone except Tom.

Always the complete sucker, I returned to the attack.

'Whatever his faults,' I said, 'he *can* play the guitar. Why are you so hard on him?'

He looked at me coldly.

'Like I said, he's a bum. A drop-out. A world-owes-me-a-living kind of guy. If he's ever done a day's work, I'd be surprised.'

'It seems to me,' I said carefully, 'that it ill-behoves anyone on this island to call anyone else a drop-out. Isn't it all rather a flight from reality?'

Tom smiled thinly, his eyes like chips of ice.

'I begin to get the picture,' he said. 'That,

lady, is all any of us need — instant psycho-analysis by the expert from over the water. I take it you're here as a one-woman rescue team for your little brother.' His tone was deceptively gentle, but I was not deceived. He was about as gentle as a cougar. 'Isn't it about time you left Nick alone?' he went on. 'He's his own man now. He needs his super-intelligent, school-ma'am sister just like a hole in the head. The kindest thing you can do is to leave as soon as possible.'

There was silence between us as, utterly taken-aback, I looked at him speechlessly. I had not, then, imagined the hostility.

He drained his coffee cup and stood up.

'Perhaps you'll excuse me,' he said. 'I guess I'll have an early night.'

He said goodbye to the rest of the company who were totally unaware of what had passed between us and, to my relief, disappeared into the darkness beyond the lighted patio. I was left to mull over his words, becoming angrier by the moment. What possible right had he to speak like that? Nick and I had always been close.

I found it impossible to concentrate on Jimmy's music, though I pretended to be absorbed, feeling thankful that I was not expected to make conversation with anyone. As my anger receded, unhappiness and uncertainty took over. Finally Jimmy stopped playing and wandered over to take Tom's vacated chair, smoking the cigarette Stella had given him. She, the moment the music stopped, had grabbed Nick and dragged him over to the dart board in the corner. Phil sat puffing impassively at his pipe, taking very little notice of anything.

I smiled at Jimmy as he sat down.

'Thank you. I enjoyed that.'

'Pleasure's all mine.'

'Do you play here every night?'

'Yeah, mostly. Rest of the time I help out behind the bar.'

'Or *not* help out, as the case may be!'

'Cor, don't you start!' Jimmy grinned at me. 'Women! Gawd, you're all the same. Can't bear a chap to be sitting down doing nothing for a second.'

'Betty seems to be trying to attract your attention. Should you be helping out right now?'

'Give over, Liz! I want to talk to you. Haven't heard any news from the old country for ages.'

'Betty's looking tired.'

The pretty waitress was leaning over our table to remove an empty glass and Jimmy caught her by the wrist.

'Araminta will help her, won't you love?'

The words were spoken wheedingly, but elicited no smile from the girl. She pulled her arm away from Jimmy and flounced off towards the bar.

'Araminta!' I echoed. 'What a gorgeous name.'

'Yeah.' Jimmy looked after the girl reflectively. 'Gorgeous bird, an' all.'

'She seems a bit cross with you.'

'Everyone is, tonight. They'll get over it.' He laughed and turned his attention to me. 'You know, it really is good to see somebody different. How are things at home?' He became aware of Lew coming towards him, a thunderous expression on his face.

'OK, OK boss, I'm just coming!' He shook his head as if despairing of the unreasonable ways of employers. 'Guess I'll have to go, Liz, but I'll see you some other time. 'Bye for now.'

He left me, but I was not alone for long. Ellen came to sit beside me, and we talked amicably for a while. Her presence soothed my ruffled feelings. She was easy to talk to — warm and outgoing and humorous, and by the time George came and whisked her off to bed, I felt that at least I had made one friend on the island.

Left alone again, I turned my attention to Nick and Stella. The darts game was now nearing an end, with both of them trying over and over to score a double one to finish. Eventually Nick threw the winning dart, and by way of congratulation, Stella kissed him lingeringly on the mouth.

Nick laughingly responded, but attempted to disengage himself when the kiss became embarrassingly long. Phil appeared not to notice, or not to care if he did, and continued to smoke in silence. I wondered uncomfortably what could be going through his mind, but was suddenly so overwhelmed by exhaustion that the whole scene began to seem unreal. I went over to Nick.

'Look, don't let me break up the party,' I said. 'But I'm dead tired. It's been a long day.'

'I'm ready for bed myself,' he said. 'Come on. I'll walk you to your room.'

He said goodnight to Stella, who looked at me petulantly, obviously blaming me for removing Nick from her clutches, and taking my arm he led me away from the lights of the patio and along the dimly lit path towards the main house.

'I'm sorry I left you so much to your own devices,' he said. 'But you seemed to be looking after yourself very well.'

'I noticed you were otherwise occupied!'

Nick failed to rise to the bait.

'How did you get on with Tom?'

'Not at all. Nick, why is he so unfriendly?' I stopped at the bottom of the outside steps leading to the balcony. 'He was positively offensive.'

'That doesn't sound like Tom.' He stood looking down at me, biting his lip. 'I don't think it's anything personal. He's just . . . '

'Just what?' I asked as he hesitated.

'Oh I don't know. He's a bit worried, I think. Don't lose any sleep over it, anyway.'

'I'll try not to.' I yawned cavernously. 'Do I see you tomorrow?'

'Of course. I'm flying all day, but I'll be back about five. See you then. We'll have dinner at home tomorrow.'

He left me and I went up the stairs to my room. I felt utterly weary as I undressed and got into bed, but although I longed for sleep, my mind was in such a turmoil that, tired as I was, I found it impossible to relax. In spite of the breeze that was stirring the light curtains it was uncomfortably hot, and for the hundredth time I punched my pillows and turned them over, trying in vain to find a cool placc on which to rest my head. My thoughts went round and round.

Why had Nick come here? I found it hard to accept his explanation. Perhaps the paper work at the Embassy had bored him. I found that easy to understand. But he had already completed most of his tour there. It seemed unlikely that he would have thrown up his entire career for that reason. And did he really want me to leave? Tom did — there was no doubt about that. But why should it matter to him?

This was ridiculous! I should be awake all night at this rate. I got up and looked out of the window. The sea was shush-shushing against the shore beyond the thin belt of casuarina trees; a gentle soporific sound, one would have thought. The beach gleamed, white and empty. There was no moon, but a million stars shone in the velvety black sky and by the light of a solitary lamp at the hotel gate I could see the boats drawn up at one side, just as they were in Nick's picture. Two more — distant, insubstantial shapes — rode at anchor.

It looked cool and tranquil down there. On impulse I slipped on my towelling robe and let myself out of the louvred doors which gave on to the balcony. Silently, on bare feet, I walked to the end and down the steps.

I had been right. It was a lot cooler outside, though the powdery sand still felt warm. I walked over to the nearest boat and sat down with my back against its hull, my arms hugging my knees, trying hard to dismiss all disquietening thoughts and let the tranquility of the night seep through my weariness.

I was, I think, almost drifting off to sleep when the sound of voices jerked me awake. I strained my eyes into the blackness and made out two figures walking along the beach in my direction, parallel to the sea. I felt a sudden clutch of panic. Had I been a fool to come out here, alone at night? I knew nothing of the local people. They could be among the most lawless and violent in the Caribbean for all I knew — a friend had returned from Jamaica with horrifying stories of armed robbery and muggings. Then, as both figures came nearer I heard a familiar voice and the knot of fear in the pit of my stomach relaxed.

But what were Tom and Nick doing, walking along the beach at this hour? It must be at least two hours — maybe even more — since Tom had left the hotel, announcing his intention of having an early night. And Nick, too, said he was off to bed. Whatever the reason for their perambulations, I had no wish to come face to face with Tom again that night, and I kept very still in the shadow of the boat, thankful that my dark blue robe would not show up in the darkness.

They passed quite close to me without being aware of my presence, and seemingly with one accord they stopped on the road, looking up at the room where they presumed me to be sleeping.

Tom spoke quietly.

'You'll have to get rid of her somehow, Nick.'

'I know.' Nick sighed heavily. 'It seems hard on her, though. I wish I could explain.'

'No way!'

Looking dejected, Nick moved off in the direction of their cottage, leaving Tom standing there alone, still looking up at the window.

'Poor kid,' he said at last, so softly that I thought I must have imagined it. Was that really compassion I heard in his voice?

2

It was some minutes before I felt like moving. It hurt to have my suspicions confirmed that both Nick and Tom wanted me to leave, but there was some consolation in the fact that they both sounded regretful about it — even Tom, which I found hard to believe. Finally I got up, brushed the sand from myself, and went back to my room by the same route as I had left it.

I felt sleepy now, and was just drifting off into unconsciousness when a noise disturbed me. Wide awake in a second, I lay rigid, every sense alert. It came again — a bump, followed by a sharp tapping noise, rather like a finger nail against wood.

I sat up in bed. For a few moments there was silence, and then I heard it again. It came from the direction of the long built-in wardrobe on the right-hand side of the room.

My heart was hammering and I gazed at the closed door of the cupboard as if mesmerized. There it was again! I switched on the bedside light, but although I could now see clearly what had been shadowy before, there was nothing obviously wrong.

A particularly large bump made me gasp.

'Is — is anyone there?' I called in a voice I could hear was unnaturally high.

Silence was the only reply, but then the uneven tapping began again. With a sudden access of determination, my throat dry, I swung my legs over the side of the bed and groped for one of the shoes I had been wearing that evening. It was a white sandal with a chunky thick heel and while not nearly as heavy as I could have wished, it was a better weapon than nothing at all. I grasped it tightly and crept towards the wardrobe.

'Is anyone there?' I asked again, this time more firmly.

A bump answered me, and suddenly taking my courage in both hands, I pulled the door open, leaping backwards as I did so, the sandal lifted high above my head.

Out scuttled the most enormous crab I had ever seen. It was all of a foot across with wicked-looking pincers which it waved in my direction, its projecting eyes seeming to me, in my nervous state, the epitome of evil and obscenity. To one who (although ashamed to admit it) was filled with disgust by something as minor as a spider in the bath, it was horrifying. For a second I stood transfixed, but as it sidled towards me I leapt onto the bed with a muffled screech and sat on it with my legs tucked underneath me, still grasping the sandal convulsively.

To me it looked like something out of a horror movie as it fixed me with its unnatural gaze. Suddenly it made a move and scuttled under the bed. Frantically I rushed from the bed and flung the balcony doors wide, dashing back to the safety of the bed again as soon as I had done so. I looked wildly round the room. If only there was a pole or a stick — but of course, there was no such thing, and I finally took an empty coat-hanger from the wardrobe, grabbed a towel, and pulled the bed away from the wall where the huge crab was revealed in all its squat malevolence, its claws waving.

I flung the towel over it, and with the coat-hanger propelled it towards the open doors. Once on the threshold, I whipped the towel away and with a swipe that would have done justice to the school hockey XI, sent the crab spinning across the balcony and down the steps. Without investigating its ultimate fate, I slammed the doors shut and locked them, leaning tremblingly against them, my flesh crawling.

At last, wearily, I retraced my steps to the bed and flung myself down, now that the whole drama was over feeling slightly ashamed that one miserable crustacean had reduced me to such a state of mindless panic. Yet it *had* been huge and it *had* looked like a creature from outer space, and worst of all, I could see no reasonable explanation of how the thing could have got into the cupboard in the first place. It had certainly not been there when I had hung my dress up before going to bed, and as it was hardly capable of closing the door firmly behind itself, it was only logical to assume that someone had put it there with the object of scaring me.

As this thought occurred to me, I dragged myself from the bed yet again and made a tour of the room, looking into drawers and peering once more into the depths of the wardrobe. As far as I could see there were no more surprises in store for me that night, and I fell almost immediately into a dreamless sleep.

A ray of sunshine, falling across my eyes, woke me next morning. I drowsed for a little, adjusting myself to my whereabouts and the memory of the events of the previous night, but this proved such a disturbing exercise that I was soon wide awake.

It was nine-thirty, and I could see from my window that Ellen was already stretched out on the beach beneath the hotel, soaking up the sun. It looked inviting and I resolved to have a quick breakfast and join her there.

50

The dining patio was deserted except for the pretty little waitress who was polishing the tables.

'Good morning,' I said to her. 'Am I too late for breakfast? I only want coffee and toast.'

With a silent jerk of her chin, Araminta indicated a table that was set in readiness for me, and flounced off towards the kitchen.

Something, I thought, seems to be bugging that young lady — or else she is totally unsuited by nature to deal with the public. A long time elapsed before she returned with the coffee and toast and placed them in front of me.

'Those are lovely earrings you're wearing,' I commented, determined to get some reaction from her. None came.

'They're made of shells, aren't they? Were they made here, on the island?'

'No, ma'am.' Her words were flat and expressionless.

'Can I get some like them?'

'No, ma'am.'

She turned away to continue with her tasks, and I gave up the unequal struggle. Araminta obviously had no wish to be friendly, and I applied myself to the coffee in silence.

I had almost finished when Betty appeared.

51

'Oh, there you are,' she said. 'There's been a phone call for you from the Chief of Police. He wants you to call in and see him.'

I looked at her in bewilderment.

'Me? The Chief of Police? What on earth for?'

'Gee, I don't know. He just said to tell you to call in some time soon.'

'What a nuisance! I was going to join Ellen on the beach.'

'Well, you don't have to rush — I don't suppose it's anything very important. Take your time, like everyone else on this island.'

'I think I'd rather get it over with. I shan't have a minute's peace until I know what it's all about! Is the Police Station far from here?'

'No, no distance at all. Just make a right out of the hotel and keep going. It's just past the Post Office — you can't miss it.'

'I'll go as soon as I've finished my coffee. Oh Betty — ' I suddenly remembered that I hadn't mentioned the crab. Perhaps Betty would be able to throw some light on it.

She turned in mid-flight, looking harrassed and abstracted. My story seemed to do nothing to alleviate the strain.

'A crab? In your closet? Are you sure?'

'Of course I'm sure! I chased it round the room and sent it flying down the steps. How could it have got there in the first place?'

She blinked nervously.

'I really haven't the slightest idea. We get a lot of them, you know. Being so near the beach and all.'

'Upstairs? In cupboards?'

'Well, gee Liz, what can I say? I'm sure sorry you had such a shock, but how it got there I can't imagine. I — I'll get the maids to spray with Shelltox.'

'Thanks,' I said dryly, thinking that a crab of that size looked as if it would drink Shelltox as an aperitif. But somehow, in the bright sunlight of the new day, I felt that my mountain of the night before was becoming more of a molehill by the minute.

I finished my coffee and went in search of the Police Station, making a right as Betty had instructed. The road led between high white stone walls, bright flowers waterfalling down from the gardens behind them. It was deserted except for a solitary road sweeper, and I was enchanted to hear music coming, it seemed from the empty air. As I approached the sweeper I realized that he had a transistor radio tuned to a religious programme propped in the front of his barrow, and this he interrupted from time to time, calling out 'Hallelujah' and 'Praise de Lord' as he swept up his rubbish. He broke off to wish me a cheerful good morning, to which I responded with a feeling of delight which had so far eluded me on this island.

A huge woman in a bright print dress and a little woollen hat rolled down the road towards me, a beaming smile on her face and a live cockerel under one arm.

'Hi, li'l darlin'', she hailed me, while she was still several yards away.

I laughed aloud as I responded to the greeting. It was good to feel that at least some of the inhabitants of this hitherto inhospitable island were friendly.

As Betty had promised, the Police Station was impossible to overlook. A tattered Union Jack was flying from the flagstaff, and several policemen, immaculate in navy blue uniforms and peaked caps, were just emerging from the doorway. I entered a trifle hesitantly but was at once taken in tow by a smart young constable and escorted to the office of the Chief of Police.

He was a slight man, with greying hair carefully plastered sideways to hide a bald head. He had a lantern jaw and a thin, rat-trap sort of mouth.

'Miss Marshall?' He rapped out my name as if he was on the parade ground. 'I'm Major Williamson. Good of you to come so promptly.'

'What can I do for you?' I asked.

He waved me to a chair and sat down himself, making a steeple of his hands and regarding me across the desk. Someone, I thought, once told him that he has a keen gaze. There really was no other word to describe the intensity of his pale blue eyes. Either that or he had been seeing movies about clear-eyed, incorruptible sheriffs, sent in to clean up the West. The silence between us lengthened until I began to wonder if my blouse was open too far, or I had a smut on my nose.

'Is there something wrong?' I asked at last.

'You arrived yesterday, I believe?' His voice was crisp and authoritative.

I nodded. 'That's right.'

'It seems that you neglected to fill in Form GG22A on your arrival.' He glared accusingly, but in spite of it I could not suppress a small giggle.

'Oh dear me, did I? I'm terribly sorry. There were several forms . . . '

'Can't let these things slip, you know. Bad for discipline.'

'I suppose it is. What a relief though! I thought I must have committed some dreadful crime. Is this really a Police matter?'

'Perhaps I should explain,' Major Williamson said, without a trace of a smile, 'that I wear two hats.'

For the life of me I could not prevent my gaze wandering to his high forehead, devoid — as far as I could see — of coverage.

'By that I mean that I am the Chief Immigration Officer as well as the Chief of Police.'

'*And* the Lord High Executioner?' I was determined to find out if that grim little mouth ever smiled.

He bared his teeth in a mirthless acknowledgement of my pleasantry, but said nothing. Perhaps, I thought, I had been tactless. Perhaps he *was* the executioner! He looked the kind of tyrant who might regard a hanging as a pleasant diversion. But surely the island came under British law, didn't it? Perhaps he was merely suffering the pangs of nostalgia, remembering the good old days when he held the final solution to the problem of the lawless.

'Don't want to waste your time or mine,' he said, proferring a form and a ball-point pen. 'Perhaps you would be so kind . . . must get the ends tied up, you know.'

I took the form and began to write, but having got beyond my name and passport number I looked at him, the pen in mid-air.

'But I *did* fill this in yesterday! I remember it distinctly. Your man at the airport must have made a mistake.'

'Really?' The curiously light eyes looked outraged and his eyebrows climbed up his forehead. 'You're sure? Well, never mind. Perhaps you'll fill it in anyway. I believe in keeping up with the paper work. Too much slackness about these days.'

I started to argue, but shrugged. 'Oh well, what's one form more or less.' I completed it quickly and handed it back to him.

'Thank you. And many apologies for bothering you unnecessarily.'

I got to my feet.

'Well, if there's nothing more . . .'

'Nothing at all, thank you Miss Marshall.' He put the form away in a drawer as I turned to leave.

'Staying long?' he asked in a casual voice before I had taken two paces towards the door.

I stiffened, but told myself I was getting over-sensitive about the subject of the length of my stay and forced myself to relax.

'Not long.'

'Good, good.' He rubbed his hands together briskly. 'Not much here for a young girl, you know. Funny sort of place, really. Not wise to stay too long. Wish I could get out, I can tell you.'

I looked at him in silence and then returned to sit down in the chair again.

'Major Williamson, are you telling me to leave Grand Guani?'

'My dear girl, I can hardly do that! It's entirely your own decision, whether you stay or leave. I am merely pointing out that the island is a strange place for a girl on her own.'

'I'm hardly on my own. I came to see my brother.'

'Ah yes, your brother.' He gave me his keen, farsighted look again. It seemed to imply that there was much he could tell me if he had the mind. 'Your brother would, I am sure, agree with me. There is very little to interest you here. We're hardly ready for tourists.'

'You mean it's dangerous?'

He looked affronted.

'No, no, no no!' He shuffled the papers round on his desk testily. 'Our police are the most efficient in the Caribbean. I've seen to that.'

'Then — then what? I don't understand.'

'A word to the wise, Miss Marshall — a word to the wise, that's all. You'd be far more likely to enjoy a holiday in Barbados or Antigua, or any of the holiday resorts. Now perhaps you'll excuse me? I have rather a lot of work on hand. Bit of a flap in Whitehall about our security arrangements. Good morning, Miss Marshall.'

I stood looking at him for a moment, but he had obviously decided that the interview was at an end and had immersed himself in his report. There seemed little to be gained by prolonging the conversation.

I was in a thoughtful mood as I went out of the Police Station and continued up the main street of the little township with the idea of exploring further. So lost in thought was I that when a car drew up beside me I failed to recognize the driver who hooted to attract my attention. It was Jimmy, cigarette between his lips, looking remarkably pleased with himself at the wheel of a very smart Thunderbird.

'Hi there,' he called.

'Hallo, Jimmy. What are you doing in such a super car?'

'Smashing, isn't it? It belongs to the hotel.'

'It looks new.'

'Yeah. Lew only imported it last week. Are you going my way?'

'I don't know. I'm just exploring.'

'Great! I'll give you a tour of the island.'

I hesitated.

'Are you sure? Isn't there anything you should be doing?'

'Not a thing. I'm free as a bird.'

I hesitated no longer and got in beside him.

'Umm, this is luxurious. How long before the rust eats it away?'

'Ooh — a year, maybe, give or take a month or two. Heart-breaking, isn't it?' He grinned cheerfully.

It was not until we were driving along the almost Canaletto-like water front that I experienced a momentary spasm of misgiving. Had I been unwise to come with Jimmy, alone like this? Heaven knew I was not normally of a nervous disposition, but there seemed to be things going on in the island that I didn't know about. More people than was comfortable seemed to want me out of the place. Was Jimmy among their number?

I looked at him sideways and he intercepted the glance.

'What's the matter, love? You're not looking exactly full of the joys of spring today.'

'Maybe it's because I didn't sleep very well.'

I recounted the story of the crab once again, and this time was astounded by the fact that Jimmy's reaction was far stronger than I had expected. He slammed on the brakes, bringing us to a full stop at the side of the road in a cloud of dust, and turned to face me, his lips thinned with anger.

'What time was this? Midnight?'

'Thereabouts, I suppose. I went out on the beach, you see, after going to bed the first time.'

'And you didn't hear anything before you went out?'

'Not a thing. I'm sure I would have done, if it had been there. Jimmy, what do you know about this? Could someone have put it there?'

'It's just the sort of daft thing . . . ' his voice trailed away, and he stared straight ahead as if lost in thought, his hands gripping the wheel.

'Maybe I do have a few ideas,' he said at last. 'Anyway, don't worry about it. I'll see it doesn't happen again.'

'But who do you think did it?'

He turned to look at me and shrugged his shoulders.

'I can only guess. Don't know for sure, so I don't want to go shooting my mouth off. Just leave it to me, Liz.'

'Gladly. It was an unnerving experience.'

'I'll bet.' He put the car into gear again and drove off slowly, his grim expression softening as the engine purred over the rough road. 'Isn't this a great little bus?'

'Mm, super. Nice of Lew to lend it to you.'

'Yeah — he's all right, is Lew. Underneath that rough exterior.'

By this time we were out of the town and were driving inland along a narrow road with wooden shacks on both sides. For the most part they were small — so small that I wondered how they could possibly accommodate the numerous children that were spilling over into the flat dirt yards that surrounded them. Nothing seemed to grow in the sandy soil, but in spite of this many of the shacks were surrounded with brilliant oleanders and bougainvilleas which flourished in cans and oil drums.

'How much more picturesque poverty is in a hot climate,' I mused.

'Yeah, but it's still poverty.'

'I know. I didn't mean to minimize it. Is it very bad?'

'Bad enough. This island worries me.'

'I wouldn't have thought anything worried you!'

'Important things do, like what's going to happen to these people. I have more to do with the locals than most of the expats do, you see. Got more in common, I s'pose. They've got nothing and neither have I.'

'What brought you here, Jimmy?'

'I just drifted, by way of the States. Went to stay with me auntie who married a GI during the war, but after a couple of months she got fed up with me. I sort of got the message when she let my room to the local bank clerk and stopped feeding me!' He laughed softly, enjoying the joke. 'So then I hitch-hiked to Florida and got a job behind the bar in an

English pub — all horse-brasses and hunting horns it was, with the waitresses dressed in tartan mini-kilts. They wanted to dress me up as a Beefeater, but I wasn't having any.'

'Is that why you left?'

'No. I sort of got involved with one of the mini-kilts. She got all serious and her mum kept asking me what me prospects were, so I got a lift on a plane coming down here. There were some blokes in the bar talking about it one night, so I said to meself, right mate, here's where you scarper. So I ended up on Grand Guani. But never mind me — you're supposed to be looking at the scenery.'

Obediently, I looked out of the window. Children swarmed everywhere. Young men sat along the walls outside their homes or clustered at the door of the occasional store or bar. Music poured out into the street. Jimmy slowed down to avoid a pair of donkeys who wandered aimlessly in the middle of the road, and as the engine faded, I could hear a loud clacking noise coming from an open-fronted saloon.

'Dominoes,' Jimmy explained. 'There's no work, so some of them play all day. Real experts, they are. Slap down the tiles like lightning.'

We were leaving the populated street behind by this time and were heading north along a track which ran across the dry, sandy waste that had so disappointed me when I first arrived. The road led upward and as we topped the rise, we could see the coast spread out before us — two sweeping crescents of white sand and beyond them the incredibly blue sea, made dazzling by the sun.

Jimmy slowed down and stopped the car close to the edge of the cliff.

'Did you ever see water like it?' he asked.

I shook my head wonderingly. 'Never. Why is it so light and clear close to the shore and such a deep blue further out?'

'A difference in depth, that's all. I always think of it as being sort of friendly round here, where it's that light colour. But over the edge of the deep — well, anything could happen?'

'Sharks?' I asked.

'And everything else. Barracuda and sting ray, and wrecks of Spanish galleons, and skeletons of sailors with thousands of little coloured fishes swimming in and out of their eyes.'

I shuddered. 'Jimmy, please! Curb the imagination, if you don't mind.'

Jimmy laughed. 'It's difficult, when you've got one like mine. Divers say it's a magic world down there. You ask Tom. The way they talk about it really gets me — the Edge of the

Deep. Sounds creepy and mysterious, doesn't it?'

'It's a lovely colour from up here. Have you been down?'

'Yeah, once.' He chuckled as if the memory amused him. 'Tom lent me his gear — or shall we say I borrowed it? Don't know why he was so mad. I didn't do it any harm.'

'You mean you took it without asking?'

'Well, he wasn't there to ask, was he? Gone to Miami, hadn't he? Cor, he didn't half blow his stack when he got back.'

'I'm not surprised,' I said faintly, beginning to feel the smallest stirring of sympathy for Tom's attitude towards Jimmy. 'After all, it is his livelihood.'

'Now don't you start! I had enough of that from Tom, and it's all over and done with weeks ago.' He was smiling and quite unrepentant. 'Anyway, I enjoyed it, and that's the main thing. That's what it's all about.'

'I agree, as long as no one else gets hurt.'

'See, you *are* getting at me!' All at once his face seemed to change. It grew chubbier, his upper lip lengthened and he leaned forward confidentially.

'What we need, my friends,' he said in a flat, slightly northern accent, 'is a land fit for the layabouts to drink in. All the working man wants at the end of the day . . . '

I burst out laughing.

'It's Harold Wilson! How on earth do you do it?'

His expression underwent a further change. He bared his teeth in a wide smile and his shoulders heaved with laughter.

'Heath!' I guessed, before he could say anything. 'Jimmy, you're a genius. Why aren't you cashing in on this?'

He turned himself into Muhammed Ali on the instant. 'Yeah, I'm the greatest! Unfortunately,' he added, returning to his own voice, 'that isn't true. People like me are ten a penny at the moment — haven't you seen them on the box? Besides, I haven't got the stomach for it. Me mum and dad were in show business — still are, sometimes, when Dad can get a job as the back end of a horse or something in panto, and it's a hell of a game. No glamour in it. Just scruffy old lodgings and mean, penny-pinching landladies.'

'Did you travel round with them?'

'When I was very small. But when I got to school age, I went to stay with me gran in London. Great old girl, she was.'

'And you never wanted to follow in their footsteps?'

'You must be joking! It's a mug's game — but mind you, so's any kind of work. It's all a mug's game.'

'There must be something you'd enjoy. You can't drift forever.'

'I know what you're thinking. 'Time you settled down, young man.' ' He adopted a mincing tone. 'I guess maybe you're right at that. But I'm in no hurry. I'm enjoying life just the way it is.' He was silent for a moment, staring unseeingly into the distance. 'Funny though, isn't it? I guess we're all more than one person. There's a part of me that longs for the security I never had. You know — a little cottage with roses round the door and a loving little chick to welcome me home.'

'Stop it,' I pleaded. 'You're breaking my heart.'

He threw back his head and laughed.

'Don't spoil my best scene. But how about you, Liz? Are you staying long?'

'Oh no!' I looked at him with dismay. 'Don't you start. Everyone seems anxious to know when I'm leaving.'

'I didn't mean it that way! It was just an innocent question.'

'Yes, I'm sure it was, Jimmy. But it's true. Even the Chief of Police seems to think I ought to go.'

'What, the Galloping Major? Him with the mouthful of plums? You don't want to take any notice of him. He can't go to the toilet without writing a report to Whitehall afterwards. Cor, no wonder we lost the Empire.'

I laughed.

'Oh bless you Jimmy, you *are* doing me good. I was beginning to lose my sense of proportion.'

'You never want to do that, love. Well, on with the conducted tour.'

'I've been meaning to ask. What are those two little islands I can see?'

'Just islands — uninhabited ones. The first one is Conch Cay and the other one a bit farther off is called Baker's Cay. He was one of the early governors, I think. There's nothing on them — just rock and scrub, like this. People go there for picnics.'

'Have you been there?'

'I went to Conch, but not to Baker's. I'll get there one day. It's funny, you know, being on a desert island. Sort of weird. Lovely shells, there are.'

'Must be great. Where are you taking me now?'

'Yeah — time we were getting on. We'll go down Snobs Alley. That's what I call it, anyway.'

'Is that where the rich Americans live?'

'That's right.'

We drove off along the road which curved slightly inland but kept parallel to the cliff.

'See that house?' Jimmy asked. 'Smashing isn't it? Belongs to some people called Vanbrugh. He made his money out of funeral parlours. Never-ending supply of customers, see. Maybe that's the business for me.'

'You'd wake up any corpse. Who lives in that Spanish-looking place?'

'A guy called Tony da Costa. Funny guy. He tries to be friendly, but the islander's don't like him. He brought down all the builders and electricians and that from the States when he built his house and the Guanians have never forgiven him.'

'That must have cost him a packet.'

'You're not kidding. But he's loaded — he couldn't care less. He's got a smashing girl friend. Well, secretary, they call her, but everyone knows she's his bird, really. Don't know how she stands him.'

'Maybe all that money helps.'

'I s'pose that's it.'

They had left the houses behind them now and were driving downhill out of sight of the sea. I could see the airport runway down on the left and beside it the expanse of water I had noticed before.

'Those are the old salinas,' Jimmy told me. 'They used to make the salt there. All useless now. Poor little old Grand Guani.'

Ahead were the shacks and houses which

meant that wc were nearing the little town again.

'Well, thanks for the tour,' I said. 'I really appreciated it. I'd never have seen so much on my own.'

'I live to serve,' he said grandly. 'Oh Lor', there's Lew outside the hotel.'

His smile had an apprehensive air as he came to a halt outside the Inn, which was more than justified by the furious expression on Lew's face as he came towards them.

'Where the hell have you been?' His anger was directed towards Jimmy, but I felt that I, too, had been to blame for his absence from the hotel and hastened to explain.

'Jimmy's been showing me around the island . . .'

'Get your ass out of that driving seat,' shouted Lew, purple in the face with rage, 'and don't ever let me catch you in it again. Who the hell gave you permission to drive my car?'

Jimmy put up his hands in mock surrender, his equanimity fully restored.

'OK, OK Boss, cool it, will you? I've been keeping one of the guests happy. Public relations, they call it.'

'You no-good bum, you've slept your last night in my hotel! Pack your bags and get out.'

He wrenched the door open and attempted to pull Jimmy bodily from the driving seat, but Jimmy managed to evade him neatly and stepped out under his own steam.

I felt embarrassed and angry. I opened the door on my side and left the car quickly, leaving the two men to their wrangle and heading towards the bar in search of a cooling drink. It was too bad of Jimmy. He had definitely given me to understand that he had Lew's permission to borrow the car and had no duties at the hotel, and I felt humiliated at being put in such an awkward position by him. And not so much as an apology to Lew, either! What an odd character he was. So thoughtful and amusing one moment, yet so utterly irresponsible the next.

There had been a small influx of visitors from a yacht, and poor Betty was behind the bar looking more harrassed than usual. I ordered an iced coke and retired to a corner of the patio to drink it in solitude, looking with interest at the newcomers. I had only been there a few moments when Jimmy sauntered in, the inevitable cigarette pasted to his lips, looking as insouciant as ever. He grinned over in my direction and gave me an enormous wink before taking his place behind the bar, relieving Betty who scuttled away to the kitchen.

When all had been served and there was a momentary lull, he wandered over to my table, open beer can in hand.

'You are a wretch,' I said. 'That was a very naughty thing to do.'

'Yes, miss. Sorry, miss.' He looked completely unabashed. 'Nice little drive though, wasn't it?' He sat down at my table.

I looked at him with exasperation.

'Honestly Jimmy, you're incorrigible! Doesn't anything bother you? Even not knowing where you're going to sleep tonight?'

He laughed. 'I know all right; I'll stay right here. Betty wouldn't throw me out, whatever Lew says. I'm really quite useful to her, when I feel like it. Besides, there's no one else.'

I shook my head at him.

'I do believe you're really rather ruthless.'

'What me? Ruthless? Get off! I just don't worry, that's all. Everyone is too uptight! What if they do throw me out? I've been chucked out of better pubs than this.' He leant towards me confidentially. 'Want my advice, Liz? Loosen up a bit. Stop taking life so seriously.'

'But you let them down again Jimmy, don't you see?'

'Well . . . ' he took a long pull at his beer. 'All come out in the wash, I expect.' He dismissed the subject. 'What are you going to do now? Have a swim? There's still time before lunch. I'd come with you, only I'm so conscientious, I have to stay here and work.' He had put on his mincing, self-righteous tone, and in spite of myself I couldn't help laughing.

'Oh, you're hopeless! Well, I suppose I'll see you later. If you're still here, that is.'

'You wanna bet? Stay cool, baby!' He flapped a hand at me and went back to take his place behind the bar as if he hadn't a care in the world. As I suppose he hadn't.

3

I surveyed the empty beach, now shimmering in the noon-day sun.

'A question,' I said to myself, 'of mad dogs and Englishmen.'

Ellen had obviously betaken herself somewhere cooler, but the water looked inviting and I wasted no more time before diving in. It was only fractionally less warm than the air temperature — none of the icy shock that one experiences at home — but it was nevertheless refreshing, and I swam about idly for a while, enjoying the play of light which dappled the sandy floor of the ocean and delighting in the shoals of tiny, silvery fish which passed underneath me. It was a calming and relaxing exercise and for a few brief minutes I forgot all my doubts and uncertainties, but the moment I stretched out on the sand in the shade of the casuarina trees, all my worries came flooding back.

Why had Major Williamson made such a point of advising me to leave the island? The more I thought about the episode in the Police Station, the more I felt certain that the form I had allegedly neglected to fill in was a totally fabricated reason for getting me to go there. The sting had been in the tail. Major Williamson wanted me out.

But *why*? I longed to be able to talk the problem over with a sympathetic listener and brooded miserably over the unkind fact that Nick, always a ready confidant, seemed the last person I could now approach. What could have changed him so drastically? There was, of course, one obvious answer to that. Tom Channing.

Tom was older than Nick — older by at least six years, but more than that, he seemed tougher and more experienced. Whatever was going on, Tom played the leading role. 'You'll have to get rid of her,' Tom had said on the beach the night before, and Nick, albeit reluctantly, had agreed.

They were obviously involved in something that had to be kept from me. Something illegal perhaps?

Oh, come *on*, I said to myself. Admittedly Nick appears to have changed. He's secretive, he wants to get rid of me, he makes an uncharacteristic play for an older married woman; but nothing could really make me believe he could be involved in something shady. Besides, I reasoned, whatever he's up to, Major Williamson knows about it — and however unattractive a personality he may be, his integrity could hardly be called in question. He seemed to me the sort of fanatic who would be shot at dawn rather than betray the principles he believed in, like keeping up with the paper work and setting a good example to the natives. And no doubt, protecting the Little Woman.

Would he, perhaps, be the sort who would think that it was hardly cricket to involve a young and innocent girl in any unpleasantness, regardless of the sins of her brother? And taking the thought a step further, wouldn't he try to get rid of the girl before any unpleasantness occurred? In other words, was he aware of whatever Nick and Tom were doing, but not necessarily a party to it? So many questions, all totally unanswerable. But one thing was clear. Tom Channing was behind it. Tom was calling the shots.

A scattering of sand across my legs interrupted these disquieting thoughts and I sat up abruptly. I was more than a little shattered to find that the man I had cast as villain of the piece was standing looking down at me, hands on his hips, clad in his working rig of the briefest of tattered shorts.

'Hi,' he said.

Could that possibly be uncertainty I could see in his face? Not Tom, surely. I nodded at him coolly without speaking.

'I was hoping to see you. May I?' He indicated the sand next to me, but without waiting for my assent, sat down beside me.

'I — er — guess I owe you an apology, Liz.'

'Yes?'

'I gave you a pretty rough ride last night — said some unkind things. Guess I must have hurt you.'

He swallowed hard as if he found the words difficult, and I guessed he was not a man who found it easy to apologize.

'I had the wrong idea about you,' he went on, as I said nothing. 'Nick put me straight after we left the hotel last night. I mean, he'd mentioned about his family always putting him down and I kind of assumed you ran with the herd. The atmosphere I walked into at the cottage yesterday afternoon didn't do much to correct the impression. Belive me, I'm sorry.'

'That's all right,' I said, simply because there was nothing else to be said. Besides, such a diffident Tom Channing was positively unnerving. 'I know I was a bit to blame myself. Sometimes I say things that sound quite different from the way I intended.'

'Americans tend to over-react to the cool, upper-class English bit.'

I was horrified.

'Is that the way I seemed to you? Honestly,

I'm not that way inside.'

'I know that now.'

'So Nick told you about his family?' I mused. 'Now he has always reacted far too violently to them. They were never as hard on him as he was on himself.'

Tom looked at me with understanding.

'Yeah, I can see that. It explains quite a lot about him.'

'Tom, what is he doing here?' I couldn't resist taking advantage of this new feeling of confidence between us. 'I know he wants me to leave — I know you both do.' I was struck by a sudden thought. 'It wasn't you who put the crab in my room, was it?'

He looked mystified, and I was inclined to believe, as I told my story for the third time, that he was as puzzled as I was myself.

'And then there's Major Williamson,' I went on. 'He hauled me into the Police Station this morning on a trumped up errand and gave me a very obvious warning to leave the island.

'He did *what*?' He whipped round to face me, with an expression of horrified disbelief. 'Oh, my *Gahd*!' He clutched his head wildly.

'Tom, will you please explain. You want me to go. Why should you be so astounded that Major Williamson wants the same thing?'

He shook his head wordlessly.

'I can't explain, Liz.'

My exasperation mounted.

'Oh no, of course you can't! No one can explain a thing. I'm totally at sea — not only at sea, but floundering.' I flung out an arm and pointed towards the horizon. 'I feel as if I'm out there, on the edge of the deep, not knowing what's underneath me.'

'Liz, please!' He leaned towards me, a hand on my arm, his voice soft and pleading. 'You must accept some things on trust. It really would be better if you left the island — better for Nick and better for you. Nick will explain just as soon as he's able.'

'But why can't you tell me now? Is it something you're both ashamed of? Something illegal, perhaps? Is that why the Major wants me out of the way, so I won't be involved in what's going on as well as my brother? Is he trying to protect me? Because if he is, Tom, he must be on to — to whatever it is. He must know all about it.'

Tom's expression was unreadable. He looked away from me for a moment, his eyes narrowed in thought, and then he turned to me again.

'I think you're right. All the more reason for you to leave as soon as possible.'

My throat suddenly felt dry, and an icy hand seemed to be squeezing my heart.

'Then it *is* something illegal?'

He looked down and idly drew a pattern in the sand, but I had the impression that his thoughts were racing.

'What are you going to do about it?' he asked. 'Turn us in?'

'My own brother? Of course not. Besides, I haven't a clue what it's all about. All I know is that you have a lot to answer for. Nick would never have got into this on his own.'

He nodded, looking sardonically amused.

'That's probably true. But don't get too steamed up about it, honey. It's a sort of one-off thing — an episode, that's all. I don't think even a hardened sinner like me could get good old upright Nick to take to a life of crime for ever.'

I looked out towards the horizon, feeling as if my world had crumbled about me.

'All right,' I said miserably. 'I'll leave tomorrow.'

I could feel Tom relax beside me.

'You've made the right decision.'

'But I'm going to try to get Nick to come too.'

'You're welcome to try.'

'Oh, you're so . . . ' Words failed me.

'So what?'

'Cold. Calculating. You must manipulate my poor brother like a puppet on a string.'

He howled with laughter.

'You do him an injustice! Your poor brother is well able to take care of himself, believe me. And as for being cold . . . ' he looked me over, as if for the first time registering the fact that I was young and female and reasonably shapely. 'Honey, you are so wrong. Why don't I fix you a sandwich back at the cottage so that we can get better acquainted? You have the wrong idea about me.'

'Thanks, but no. I'll go back to the hotel — I don't feel like eating much. Shouldn't I see about booking my passage tomorrow?'

'Don't worry I'll fix it.'

'You're too kind,' I said dryly. I stood up, picking up my towel. 'I believe I'm dining with you tonight.'

'So I hear. I caught us a fish this morning.'

'Don't you do any real work?'

'Hey!' Tom looked outraged. 'Sure I work! I give diving instructions and take tourists out — I'll be out all afternoon with that family from the hotel. It's just that I'm slack right now. The busy season starts in a few months when the weather turns cold up north.'

'If only you'd stick to diving!'

He looked amused. 'There's no bread in it, honey! Sure I can't give you lunch?'

'What's a sandwich without bread?' I

81

asked. It wasn't a very good joke, but he laughed anyway.

I hadn't intended to sleep, but drowsiness overcame me after I had, after all, eaten a brief snack at the bar.

Voices of children on the beach woke me. My pillow was damp, my hair sticking to my forehead and plastered uncomfortably to the nape of my neck. The thought of another swim was inviting, and in a few minutes I was out on the sands which now presented a very different picture from the deserted beach where I had swum before lunch. Mothers with children were sitting under the trees and the shallows were full of bobbing heads. A group of little local boys were diving from the breakwater, shrieking and laughing as they pushed each other under.

I had a more prolonged swim this time, feeling the water once again soothing away much of the strain. By the end of it, I felt almost resigned to the fact that I was to leave the island so soon, but more than ever determined to persuade Nick to leave with me. Once on dry land I fished around in my beach bag for my watch and strapped it on my wrist again. Too early yet to find Nick at home — he had said he wouldn't be in until after five. But as soon as I had given him time to return from his last flight, I was determined to swoop in to the attack.

I stretched out my towel in the sun and sat down on it. There was no room now under the trees, but the heat of the sun was not quite so fierce as it had been earlier, and I gloried in the feel of it. Others, too, were soaking it up, and I wondered how long it would take me to cultivate the sort of tan I could see all around me. That girl over there, for instance, who was talking to Ellen Myers. She was quite the loveliest shade of golden-copper I had seen.

Ellen caught sight of me and waved, calling to me to go and join them. Gladly I did so, being heartily tired of my own thoughts.

The girl with her was introduced as Donna Petersen, whose Nordic forebears were no doubt responsible for her ash-blonde beauty. At close quarters she was even more attractive than had at first appeared. Her eyes were a deep, smoky blue over an appealing tip-tilted nose. She acknowledged the introduction with a friendly smile.

'I was just wondering how long it would take me to cultivate a super tan like yours,' I said.

Donna laughed. 'Oh, I guess I was born with this. I've lived in Florida almost all my life, so I'm no stranger to sunshine.'

'Are you on holiday?' I asked.

'No, I work here. I'm secretary to a man called Tony da Costa — he's something of a collector. He's cataloguing all his coins and stamps and objets d'art.'

So this was the 'smashing bird' that Jimmy had mentioned! He had not exaggerated.

'I passed his house this morning,' I said. 'It looks quite a show place.'

'It's all of that, and of course the view is out of this world. But there are disadvantages of living upon the North Ridge.'

'Hard to imagine what they can be,' Ellen put in.

'Well, for one thing there's no place to moor his boat. That's Tony's, the big white cabin cruiser out there.' She pointed to one of the two boats riding gently at anchor just off the beach. 'It's much too rough and rocky over on our side. And I always come down here to swim. The beaches on the north side are dirty. All the driftwood and refuse in the ocean seems to wind up there.'

'Tony should build a swimming pool,' Ellen said.

'He just might do that. There's a problem with the siting of it, though.'

'Is the work interesting?' I asked.

Donna pulled a face. 'Not very, but at least it allows me to work down here. I just love it on the island.'

'As Nick says, it does have a charm that isn't immediately obvious.'

'He's right. It's not just scenic beauty that appeals, but the quiet leisureliness of life. Does your brother like it?'

'He seems to. Probably you know his views better than I do, as I haven't seen him for so long. Everyone seems to know everyone else here.'

She shrugged. 'Oh, I know him, of course, but our paths hardly cross.'

'Talking of Nick,' Ellen put in. 'He phoned George today about our Haiti trip. He says he can fly us on Saturday, as long as we come back the following day. Why don't you come with us, Liz? There'll be a spare seat on the plane, and plenty of room at the hotel this time of year. We'd love you to be our guest.'

'Oh Ellen, I wish I could,' I said regretfully, 'but something's come up. I have to leave Grand Guani tomorrow.'

'Tomorrow! But that's crazy — you've only just come. Donna, tell her she can't leave so soon! Why, you'll miss Tony's party as well as the Haiti trip.'

'I can't tell you how grateful I am for the offer, but really I must go.'

'But to come such a long way!' Ellen appealed to Donna again. 'Go on Donna, tell her she must stay. Tell her about Tony's party.'

'No doubt Liz knows her own business best,' Donna said gently, smiling at me. For one moment I could have sworn there was a deep understanding in her blue eyes, but I dismissed the thought as ridiculous. No one apart from Nick and Tom could possibly know why I was leaving.

'What's all this about a party?' I asked, hoping to distract Ellen from pursuing the subject of my stay further.

'It's Tony's birthday,' Donna explained. 'It's become a kind of tradition. He can't be bothered to entertain much, so every year he has this enormous wing-ding and pays off everyone in one enormous splurge. I haven't been here for any of the others, but I gather that everyone on the island goes and it's regarded as the party of the year. Too bad you can't make it.'

I agreed, but pleaded once again that urgent business at home made it necessary for me to leave. Glancing at my watch I saw that five o'clock was rapidly approaching, and began to gather up my things.

'I think I'll go and take a shower,' I said, getting to my feet. 'It's been nice meeting you, Donna.'

'Have a good trip home if we don't meet again,' she said.

'I think I'll come back with you.' Ellen

stood up, too. 'George should be back any moment.'

We walked together across the sand and over the road which lay between the hotel and the beach.

'What a pretty girl,' I commented.

'Donna? Isn't she, though! And such a sweet person, too. You know,' Ellen went on, after a moment's pause. 'I worry about that girl.'

'Why? She seems very happy here.'

'Oh sure, she seems happy. But I'd hate to think of her getting in too deep with that Tony da Costa. He isn't at all what you would call a *nice* man! We've known him for some time now — ever since we began coming down here, and there's always some other pretty girl working for him. Secretaries, he calls them, but I don't know . . . some of them haven't looked or behaved in the least like secretaries. Now Donna is utterly different. Far too good to be mixed up with a man like that.'

'Don't you think it could be just a job to her?' I asked.

Ellen looked doubtful.

'I'd like to think so! Oh, I guess I'm just a silly old biddy without a chick or child of my own — I tend to get all maternal about young people. No doubt Donna is quite able to take care of herself. I just wouldn't like a daughter of mine living in the same house with that man, that's all.'

She saw George from afar and went off to meet him, leaving me to shower and change into a brief skirt and sun-top. I looked at my watch once more and decided that I now had a good chance of finding Nick at home without, I devoutly hoped, Tom Channing's disconcerting presence. I stopped in my tracks. Why should he disconcert me? I resolved to have no more of it.

I found the gate of the cottage open. Good, I thought. Nick must be home. I had adopted the universal habit of walking bare-footed, and so made no sound as I approached the tiny front door and let myself in. I was about to call and announce my presence, when my eyes fell on a towel and beach-bag, gaily striped in shades of blue, that were set down on one of the chairs. I had seen those objects before, only a few minutes ago.

I hardly had time to wonder what Donna's things were doing in the cottage — hadn't she said that she hardly knew Nick? — when I heard a sound from the bedroom; a long, intimate sigh that was almost a groan.

'Oh, darling,' came Nick's voice, husky and tender and quite unlike his normal tones. 'What a hell of a situation!'

'Oh Nick, I know, I know. But it can't be much longer, can it? Not much longer, darling.'

'If you only knew how much I love you!'

As silently as I had come to the cottage, I fled.

4

Much to my annoyance, Tom was approaching the cottage by the time I deemed it safe to make a second entrance, and therefore there was no opportunity to talk to Nick on his own.

Nick's relief was obvious when I announced my intention of leaving the following day.

'Did you manage to book me a seat?' I asked Tom.

'No trouble at all.'

'What goes on?' Nick asked. 'What made you decide to go?'

I looked at Tom. He could provide the explanations.

'I told Liz everything,' he said.

Nick, on his way across the room to me with a cold drink in his hand, swung round to face his friend.

'You did *what*?'

'Cool it,' Tom said quietly. 'I merely told Liz that our little operation here doesn't exactly enjoy the full blessing of the law. Is that or is that not correct?'

Nick looked at him in silence.

'Correct,' he admitted at last. 'I suppose.'

'And Liz,' Tom went on, 'being the sensible girl she is, not wanting to get mixed up in anything shady, agreed to leave at once.'

'But I don't like it,' I burst out. 'Nick, for heaven's sake, come to your senses and come home with me. It surely isn't too late to get out of this mess.'

Nick smiled a little ruefully and came to sit down beside me.

'Look,' he said, 'I'm in this for better or worse. I can't leave now. I'm sorry you came just at this moment when things are . . . ' he stopped, searching for the right expression.

'Coming to the boil?' Tom supplied helpfully.

I shot him a furious glance.

'You got him into this,' I said angrily. 'Nick was fine until you came along.'

'My decision to come here was made before I met Tom,' Nick said quietly. 'I told you that before.'

'Oh!' I leaned my head back in the chair and closed my eyes. 'I don't understand a single thing about the situation. And Nick — I know it seems unimportant to you, but what the hell am I to tell Dad? That you're carving out a new career for yourself down here? Or that you'll soon be home? Or what?'

'Oh, tell him I'm a beachcomber, living in a

grass hut with a native girl, and that my hair is down to my shoulders, and I have dirty nails. And you can add that on the rare occasions when I wear trousers, my hands are *always* in my pockets.'

'Make a joke of it if you like, Nick, but he's getting old and he worries about you. I'm beginning to think you don't deserve it.'

He had the grace to look shamefaced.

'I'm sorry! Just tell him I'm flying and I'm happy. I know!' he sat up straight as if suddenly struck by inspiration. 'Tell him I'm in line for Chief Pilot.'

Tom, who had his nose in a glass of beer, almost choked.

'What's so funny?' I asked innocently.

'Not really funny,' Nick said. 'Tom has a sick sense of humour. You see, there's only Phil and myself flying just now. Phil's senior — he's been here for several years — but he's such a god-awful pilot we expect him to write himself off at any moment. Hence the possible vacancy.'

'Poor Stella,' I said.

'Ah yes.' Nick's voice was meditative. 'Stella.'

'Nick,' I began tentatively, and then stopped.

'Hmm?'

'Well, it was obvious last night that you and

Stella — I mean, I couldn't help noticing that you were making a play for her, or vice versa.'

'The vice couldn't be more versa, I assure you.'

'Maybe. But you were going along with it pretty happily. I know it's none of my business, but what *is* going on?'

'Not nearly as much as Stella would like to go on,' Tom said, coming to Nick's rescue. He and Nick exchanged amused glances. 'Don't shed any tears for her. She changes her young men like she changes her underwear.'

'It's — it's sort of shattering when you feel that a person you've known all your life seems to have turned into someone quite different.'

Nick looked a bit sad at that, but said nothing.

'I met an awfully nice girl on the beach this afternoon,' I said, hopefully sounding casual. 'Much more your type than Stella, I would have thought, but she didn't seem to know you very well. Her name was Donna. I gather she works for someone called Tony da Costa.'

'Let me give you a refill.' Nick stood abruptly and took my glass over to the kitchen counter. 'I know who you mean,' he said, his back to the room. 'She's quite a looker.'

He poured the drink in silence.

'We hardly ever see each other,' he said, as

he crossed the room towards me again. 'I imagine she's more than occupied with da Costa. Hey Tom, when are you going to start cooking? We're frying tonight,' he added in my direction. 'Tom caught a snapper this morning.'

'Patience, man,' Tom counselled. 'I'm having a shower first.'

He finished his drink and went off in the direction of the bedroom, leaving me alone with Nick and an uneasy silence.

'I'm sorry, Liz — believe me, truly truly sorry.'

'Then come home with me,' I urged.

Nick looked at me with exasperation.

'I can't! Won't you please get that through your head? I have to see this thing through. When it's over I can tell you everything.'

'If you're not behind bars. What's the inside of the Grand Guani jail like?'

'That's something I'll never know. Liz, we've only got one evening left — don't spoil it by nagging. The last thing I want to do is quarrel with you.'

I sighed and admitted defeat. And although I felt I had no heart for bright, superficial conversation, in spite of myself I enjoyed Tom's snapper and was even able to relax as Nick and Tom appeared to put themselves out to be entertaining. I felt sure that their stories of island life had to be exaggerated, but they were very funny, nonetheless. No place could surely be quite so crammed with characters, local or imported.

Tom was revealed in a new light as an agreeable, amusing raconteur, and I felt almost sorry when he tactfully made his excuses and left me alone with Nick, presumably so that we could indulge in family talk without risk of embarrassment.

But the tempo of the evening slowed down with his departure. Left alone with Nick, all my depression returned and it was quite early when I said goodnight and went back to the hotel, saddened and worried. I would never have thought such a breakdown of communication possible between Nick and myself.

After a tour of the bedroom to make sure that there were no unwelcome intruders, I read for a while, but once again there was too much on my mind for me to sleep. Finally I gave up the struggle and went outside again, into the velvety, murmurous night — cool and welcoming after the hot hotel room.

I made my way across the powdery sand towards the boat which had sheltered me the night before, and was halfway towards it when the sudden glow of a cigarette end in the darkness made me check my footsteps. Someone was there before me. I stood irresolutely for a second, then turned to retrace my footsteps when a voice stopped me.

'Liz?'

I peered into the blackness and took a few tentative steps.

'Tom! You gave me quite a shock — I didn't expect anyone to be here. What are you doing?'

'The same as you, I guess. Not sleeping. Come and visit a while.'

I continued across the sand and joined him, my back resting against the boat.

'Why can't you sleep?' Tom asked.

'Need you ask? Too many unanswerable questions.'

'Don't worry about Nick, Liz. I'll look out for him.'

'Why should I trust you?'

I felt him shrug beside me in the darkness.

'I guess there's no reason why you should.'

'How long have you known him, Tom?'

'About five months. Long enough to know he's a good man to have on the same team.'

'What did he tell you about his family?'

'Just that he has this complex about not measuring up. Look — I've said I'm sorry about last night!'

'It worries me, Tom,' I said hesitantly. 'I can't help feeling that whatever he's into, it's to *show* the rest of us — to get at Father, somehow. He's trying to prove something. I don't think I ever realized before how he felt about not measuring up, as you call it. I thought he'd got over that years ago. Surely it's a bit immature, isn't it? To go on feeling that way?'

'Stop worrying about him. He's free, white and twenty-one, and the master of his own fate — and believe me, not as immature as all that. Most of us have the odd hang-up about something. What about you, Liz? Will you go straight back to England or back to your friends in Florida?'

I gave a short laugh.

'I'm afraid my friends in Florida were rather a myth. I went to stay with a man I met in London, but it didn't work out. He was as pleased to see the back of me as Nick and you are.'

'Hey!' He laid an arm along the back of my shoulders and turned me to face him. 'Don't put yourself down like that!'

'How can I help it? It's enough to make any girl feel she ought to change her deodorant when all anyone wants to do is get her on the next plane. Maybe there's something my best friends won't tell me!'

Tom laughed gently.

'Liz, you're beautiful! It's too bad Nick and

97

I have to hurt you like this.' His arm tightened around me. 'Tell me about this creep in Florida.'

For a moment I hesitated, but only for a moment. There was a comfortable anonymity about sitting there in the darkness with a man I would never see again after tomorrow, with the sea murmuring away in the background; a man, moreover, who appeared to listen with sympathy and understanding when I told him about the visiting academic with whom I seemed to have so much in common.

'We used to talk for hours,' I told him, 'about — oh, you know, things like Ingmar Bergman's impact on the theatre and Is This the End of the Era of the Novel as we Know It.' I was guying myself a bit, and he acknowledged the fact by a breath of laughter.

'But somehow,' I went on, 'when I saw him on his home territory, it all went sour. He seemed such a poseur — a kind of two dimensional figure in a bad play. And I think I seemed an inhibited provincial. Intellectually dishonest, he told me.'

'You didn't expect him to do nothing but talk about Ingmar Bergman, I hope?'

'No, of course not! But I did expect a little more — finesse. A little less absorption with Wayne Everett. Oh, no doubt I was greatly to blame. I seem to have a talent for messing up relationships.'

'So you didn't escape either?'

'What do you mean?'

'You have your hang-up, too. Feelings of inadequacy. That father of yours has a lot to answer for.'

'Oh no, it isn't his fault! I think I was born with quite a good brain, but not much common sense. It helps if the two go together.'

Tom laughed again.

'You were also born very beautiful — and this Wayne guy sounds a real pill. You're well out of it, in my opinion. Don't give him another thought.'

'I won't,' I promised, and was happily silent for a few moments, listening to the sound of the sea and feeling comfortably aware of Tom's arm around my shoulders. Temporarily I had forgotten completely about his illegal activities, whatever they might be.

'What makes you like you are?' I asked him.

'How I am?'

'Well,' I thought about it. 'It's difficult to sum up. Sure of yourself, I suppose. A bit hard, perhaps; wrong about some things, maybe. But basically — self-accepting.'

'Self-accepting?' He thought about it. 'Doesn't one have to be? Maybe two years in Vietnam helped.'

'Now it's your turn to talk. Tell me about it!'

'Honey, that would take all night.'

But just the same, he made the attempt and the sky was perceptibly lightening towards dawn before we finished talking. It was a strange night, and one which neither of us wanted to end. The chances were good that we would never meet again, and for this reason, perhaps, we revealed more of ourselves to each other than we would have done in normal circumstances.

'I must go,' I said at last. 'We shan't get any sleep at all at this rate.'

Tom kissed me lightly once, and then again, not quite so lightly.

'You're not going to be easy to forget, Liz. I'll see you tomorrow, before you go, but this is really goodbye. Will you think of me kindly, in spite of everything?'

I leant against him for a moment, thinking how odd it was that I had talked more to this stranger — really talked — than to my own brother, the companion of my youth.

'Yes,' I said at last, looking up at him. 'For some curious reason, I will think of you kindly.'

He kissed me again; and that time it wasn't light at all.

5

The bill was paid, the bags packed. I sat in the shade of the patio attempting to read as I waited for Nick to come back from his morning flight, but concentration was diffi-cult. I felt light-headed and strangely detached from my surroundings — no doubt attributable to lack of sleep. But in no way did I regret those hours on the beach with Tom. I had the feeling that when I looked back on my short stay in Grand Guani, those would be the ones I would remember with most pleasure.

The effect of my light-headedness was to make my surroundings stand out with startling clarity. The sandy coloured lizard, motionless except for his pulsating throat, was outlined against a yellow hibiscus flower like a cardboard cut-out. In the sunshine outside, a humming bird nosed hungrily into the centre of a frangipani, its tiny wings beating so rapidly that it, too, seemed stationary. As a background to all this I was aware of Jimmy whistling softly as he checked the level of bottles in the bar; the whoosh of the brooms of the two maids who were sweeping the patio and the path outside, and the sound of metal striking metal, as Truman, the hotel handyman, went about his business of fixing and mending. I lazily considered reminding him that the fan in my room was still out of action, but dismissed the idea. It would mean stirring from my chair — a prospect that filled me with lethargy. Let the next occupant make his own complaints. I would be gone soon enough.

I looked at my watch. Nick was late. He had said that he'd fixed an early finish to his day and would be back by ten-thirty so that he could spend with me the little time that remained — but here it was, after eleven, and still no sign of him. I thought little of it. There was still plenty of time before the plane left at two thirty, and short though my stay had been, I was aware that on this island time was something that had little importance.

I had been waiting to have a drink until Nick arrived, but my thirst was such that I summoned all my energy and managed to walk over to the bar myself.

'All ready for the off, then?' Jimmy asked, as he served me with my bitter lemon, crackling with ice.

I nodded, savouring the refreshingly acid bubbles.

'Well, you didn't stay long, did you? What's

the matter with us, then? Don't you fancy us, now you've had a closer look?'

'It's not that at all. I have to get back to work.'

He gave me a shrewd look.

'Oh yeah? I thought schools didn't start until the first week in September? There's two weeks to go yet.'

'I have things to do — preparations to make.'

'Sure you're not running away from anything?'

'Why should I be?

He shrugged.

'I dunno. It was you said people seemed to want to get rid of you.'

I leaned against the bar, drained of energy.

'Sheer imagination,' I said.

'Didn't imagine the crab though, did you?'

'No, of course not. Did you find out anything about it?'

'Just say there's someone helping me with my enquiries.'

Too many unanswered questions, I thought. I was too tired to think about them.

'Oh well,' I said vaguely. 'I don't suppose it matters.'

I drifted back to my chair, drink in hand, and lay back with my eyes closed. The whole situation, I felt, was enough to make anyone feel out of touch with reality. I felt as if I were in a glass cubicle with everyone else outside, mouthing words I couldn't understand. Nothing made sense.

For instance, why should Nick be so secretive about what appeared a very genuine attachment to Donna? Because of the possible jealousy of this Tony da Costa I'd heard so much about? Or was it something more sinister — a guilty sort of liaison between them. Some sort of a plot involving Nick, Tom and Donna, all work-together. Robbery, perhaps?

But nothing could make me believe that Nick was a thief, or Tom for that matter, not now that I knew him better. Unless . . . unless there was some sort of extenuating circum- stances; a kind of Robin Hood operation, perhaps, or the restoration of something in da Costa's possession to its rightful owner. Ellen obviously disliked him thoroughly. Perhaps *he* was the thief! Perhaps among those coins and objets d'art that Donna had mentioned there was something that didn't belong to him at all. Only something of the sort could make sense, I thought. I would never believe that it was in Nick's nature to behave in a truly immoral way.

Heavens, it was getting late! I sat up straight, wide awake. Where on earth could

Nick be? Surely, even on Grand Guani, it was unusual for him to be an hour late returning from a flight.

I finished my drink and decided to make the effort to walk over to the cottage. Perhaps I had misunderstood and was supposed to meet Nick there — though I knew that made no sense. If he had been at home, he would have come in search of me by this time.

As always the door of the cottage was unlatched and I walked in. The part-time maid had been and gone. The floors were swept, the kitchen clean, the beds made. But there was no sign of Nick.

It was all so still and silent. Only the dust motes moved in a shaft of light. Two days, I thought; just two days. No time at all, really, yet enough for me to catch a glimpse of a world I never knew existed.

Nick's picture on the wall drew me like a magnet.

'I'll ask him for it,' I thought. 'It'll always remind me of Grand Guani — the heat and the glare and the immobility of solid objects. The way things just seem to *be* in this heat. And the strangest night of my life, sitting under the stars and confiding in a perfect stranger.'

How curious it was that Nick had this talent and had been exercising it, unknown to me. How was it possible for him to have grown into such a stranger? And more important, where *was* he?

I looked at my watch again and for the first time felt a chill of apprehension. Almost ten to twelve! He must have arrived back from the morning flight by this time.

I went back to the hotel, coming face to face at the gate with Truman, the handyman. He was a tall, rangy islander, with baggy shorts and a torn vest, topped by an ancient yachting cap, and he held the gate for me as I went through.

'You lookin' for yo' brudder?' he asked with a gap-toothed smile. 'He don' reach yet.'

'No, I'm afraid not,' I said.

Betty was on the patio talking to Jimmy when I returned there, and came over to speak to me.

'Gee,' she said, 'it really is too bad you have to rush off this way. I'm real sorry you had to cut your stay short.'

'I'm sorry too,' I said. 'Betty, I'm beginning to be worried about Nick. He was supposed to have been here by ten thirty. What do you think can have happened?'

'Ten thirty?' Betty chewed her underlip nervously. 'Oh gee, that's real worrying — I mean, with him flying and all. Why don't you call the airport and see if they know anything?

106

He could have been delayed on one of the other islands.'

'Of course — how stupid of me! I should have done that ages ago.'

Relieved to have some positive course of action to follow, I went into the entrance hall of the hotel and used the telephone.

After a considerable delay and a fruitless conversation with a lady who turned out to be a cloakroom attendant, I was passed over to an employee of Guani Group Airlines, who assured me that Nick had returned from his flight over an hour before.

Then where was he? I stood by the phone for a few minutes wondering if there was any way I could contact Tom, but I remembered that he said he would be diving over the edge of the deep most of the morning, if he could get his boat started without the vital part he was still waiting for. There was no sign of him, so I could only assume he had managed to get the thing going. I wandered back to the patio and stood indecisively, wondering what I ought to do. Preparations for lunch were going forward. Should I eat while I had the opportunity, or should I wait? While I was standing there irresolutely Truman slopped past on his rubber flip-flops, and grinned at me good-naturedly.

'He don' reach yet, do he ma'am? He very late, for true.'

This time my smile was a mere token. Well meaning as he might be, I needed a running commentary from Truman at that point like the proverbial hole in the head. I would wait, I decided. There was still time in hand before the plane.

I sat down again, put my head back against the chair, and closed my eyes, fighting the panic which was slowly mounting in me.

'Liz?'

My eyes flew open as I heard my name, but it was Tom, not Nick, who was standing in front of me.

'Tom, thank heavens you've come. Where's Nick?'

'Isn't he here?'

'No, he's not — and I'm worried to death! I phoned the airport and they said he arrived back on schedule just before half past ten. What can have happened to him?'

Tom pulled up another chair and sat down close to me, his face tightening with concern. He stared thoughtfully at the ground for a moment, but then, as if making up his mind, looked up at me, forcing a smile.

'Well,' he said, 'I guess there's no cause for alarm as long as the plane has landed. Stay cool, Liz — he's just gotten delayed some place. Why don't we have some lunch? He'll be along soon, you'll see.'

'I don't feel like lunch,' I said stubbornly. 'And you're fobbing me off. How do you mean, delayed? Who or what would have delayed him, when he particularly arranged to spend my last morning with me?'

'Could be that he had something to deliver — something urgent. He does it all the time. Folks on the other islands give the pilots parcels and letters to deliver on Grand Guani. Maybe he called in on someone — stayed for a beer — you know how it is?'

'No, I don't know how it is, and I'll thank you not to treat me like a particularly retarded child of four. Tom, what has *happened* to him?'

Tom's smile, not very confident to begin with, faded altogether.

'I'll level with you,' he said grimly. 'I haven't the first cotton-pickin' idea, and that's the truth.'

'Unless he comes,' I said carefully, not wanting there to be any misunderstanding, 'I'm not leaving. You can forget it.'

'Liz, you must leave!' Tom turned to face me, his voice urgent. 'That's what Nick would want.'

'To hell with what Nick wants, or you either. I'm tired of being pushed around. I'll leave when I know my brother is safe, and not before.'

'If you miss this plane, you'll have to stay until next Tuesday.'

'I'm well aware of that. Tom, you can argue all you want,' I went on, seeing him about to protest, 'I'm just not going — not without seeing Nick first.'

He looked at me furiously, his jaw set and those grey eyes — which I had seen yesterday sparkling with warmth and good humour for the first time — had returned to their original icy state. But he must have recognized my determination, as he sighed, and made a visible effort to relax.

'Liz,' he said, his voice soft and persuasive. 'You know Nick wanted you to leave for a very good reason. Please do what he asked.'

For a moment I wavered. His pleading was hard to resist, but I had a momentary picture of my own state of mind, sitting in the plane and wondering what had happened to Nick, and I shook my head.

'No, Tom. Sorry — but there's no way I'm leaving here until Nick turns up. I won't interfere with anything. I'll stay in the hotel if you like, but I'm *not* leaving.'

He sprung to his feet and towered over me, his hands clenched in his pockets.

'God-damned *women*!' he grated. He

seemed too angry to say more, and finally shook his head with exasperation and made as if to leave.

'Tom — Tom, where are you going?'

'To see if I can rustle up that damned brother of yours before the plane leaves!'

Truman slip-slopped across from the dim reaches behind the bar to the bright sunlight outside.

'Mr Nick don' reach yet?' he grinned as he passed me. 'He sure is late, ma'am — he *sure* is late. You done been waitin' a long, long time.'

I glared at his blissfully unconscious backview as if he alone were responsible.

The lazy, languorous day slipped by, the hours passing too quickly for my liking. At a little after half past two I heard the sound of a plane overhead and knew that for good or ill I had lost all chance of leaving the island for the next few days. As three o'clock succeeded two, and four o'clock succeeded three, all without a word from either Nick or Tom, my worry increased. I never did get around to eating lunch, and by four thirty I decided to go over to the cottage and make myself a sandwich, chancing a chilly reception from Tom.

There was, however, no sign of him. I found some bread and cheese and made myself a cup of coffee, and felt better for having eaten, though nothing alleviated my all-absorbing worry about Nick's where-abouts.

Tom arrived just as I had finished washing up my cup and plate. He seemed to hesitate on the threshold as he saw me.

'Any news?' I asked.

He shook his head wearily.

'Not a thing!'

He came inside the room and slumped down in a chair, his long legs stretched before him and his arms hanging loosely.

'How can a man vanish on an island of this size?' He was speaking to himself, softly and savagely, and I didn't attempt to answer him. 'I just can't . . . ' his voice trailed away, as if he were worried beyond endurance.

'Have you eaten?' I said. 'Can I get you anything?'

'Thanks. I'd love some coffee.'

He drank the coffee and ate the sandwich I provided abstractedly, but it appeared to restore him sufficiently for him to give me some sort of a smile over the rim of his cup.

'So here you are and here you stay, huh?'

'You'd better believe it,' I said, using a phrase I'd borrowed from him. 'I'm glad you're not still angry with me.'

He set his cup down carefully.

'Honey, angry isn't the word, not any more. I'm just plain scared.'

I was scared too — had been for hours, but I hated him to confirm that I had a right to be.

'Oh Tom, so am I! What can have happened? Did you check that he arrived on time?'

'Sure. He arrived just a few minutes after ten-twenty and drove off in his car.'

'In this direction?'

'Nobody saw. He can only have taken one of two roads, and I've been down both of them. No sign of him or his car. I even checked the caves, down at the south end of the island — but again, nothing to be seen. Not that I expected him to be there.'

'What caves are these?' I asked.

'Just caves. They're quite a tourist attraction and go from one side of the island to the other, down where the land narrows to only a mile or so across. But there's no reason on earth why Nick should have gone there. Anyway, there was no sign of his car.'

We lapsed into silence. Tom was deep in thought, but I was too confused and worried to think clearly at all.

'You know,' I said at last, breaking the silence. 'While I was hanging around the hotel I sort of worked out a theory about you and Nick. About what you're doing here, I mean.'

'Oh?' Tom raised a quizzical eyebrow at me.

'It's something to do with Donna, isn't it?'

'Go on. You interest me.'

I swallowed nervously, suddenly feeling sure that I was making a fool of myself.

'I'm only guessing, of course, but I just happened to find out, quite by accident, that Nick knows Donna a lot better than he tried to make me think. They both told me they hardly knew each other — '

'Hardly *saw* each other, I think Nick said. There's a difference.'

'Yes, of course there is. But however he expressed it, he was secretive about knowing her, and knowing her very well indeed from what I could gather.'

'What makes you think that?'

I recounted overhearing Nick and Donna's tender passage in the cottage and was rewarded by the expression of total amazement that came over Tom's face.

'You look surprised,' I said. 'Didn't you know they were in love?'

'I should say not! It's enough to make me blow my mind!' He took his empty cup, and striding the length of the room with it, banged it down on the kitchen counter. 'May the good Lord preserve me from amateurs!'

'I can't see why you're so mad,' I said.

He returned to his chair and looked at me with a hint of amusement.

'I don't suppose you can,' he said. 'OK, so now we have violins playing in the background and the place strewn with hearts and flowers. What did you decide was going on centre stage?'

'I came to the conclusion that whatever you two are involved in, Donna's in on it too. And then I remembered what she said about Tony da Costa being a collector. It sounds as if he has some really valuable things.'

'So you put two and two together and decided we're planning a heist?'

'It seemed a distinct possibility.'

He looked at me as if deeply pained, but was unable to hold his grave expression for more than a second. He dropped his head in his hands and laughed.

'You *did* say it was something illegal,' I said, feeling rather injured at his immoderate mirth.

'So I did, honey, so I did.' He looked at me and smiled. 'But you're way off beam about friend da Costa.'

I leaned forward urgently.

'Please tell me, Tom. Can't you see how awful it is, not knowing? Especially now Nick is missing. At least you must have some theory about what's happened to him. I'm so sick and tired of being in the dark.'

'Theories! Sure, I have a few. But there's nothing I can think of that would keep him away for so long, unless . . . '

I looked at him swiftly, and looked away again. I didn't want him to put his fears into words.

'Please tell me,' I urged again.

'OK,' he said, after a moment's silence. 'I'll give it to you straight. We're after heroin.'

'Drugs?' I looked at him stupidly, not understanding. 'How do you mean, you're after them? You can't mean that you and Nick deal in drugs!'

'Of course not! Look, Liz — we had to get you away quickly. We were both agreed on that, because things are going to be bust wide open very soon. That's why I went along with your assumption that we were on the wrong side of the law, so that you'd turn tail and run in disgust.'

'You mean — you mean . . . ' I was so outraged, I couldn't get the words out.

'Other methods of persuasion didn't seem to be having any effect. Liz, we're not playing — this isn't a game! There are millions of dollars involved, and these guys play rough. There's already been more than one murder.

We had to get you out.'

'But to make me think . . . .'

'Try to understand! Nick would have explained afterwards.'

'Are you a policeman?'

Tom nodded. 'And Nick's on temporary assignment.'

'You certainly made a fool out of me, didn't you? And I fell for it, hook, line and sinker. What a gullible idiot you must think me! I still think it was unforgiveable.'

'But effective. We hated doing it, Liz, but we had to get you away.'

'The best laid schemes,' I said. 'I'm still here.'

'That's what worries me.'

'You'd better tell me everything now. I'm perfectly capable of keeping my mouth shut, you know. You need have no fear of that.'

'That's hardly the point. We wanted you safe, where no one could get at you.'

'Come on, Tom,' I said. 'The whole story, please.'

He looked at me as if weighing it up.

'OK then,' he said at last. 'This is it. Heroin is coming into the States via Florida. Now, most comes from Turkey via France where the raw morphine is refined. You've heard of the French Connection? Well, it's no fiction — but for one reason and another we've been able to seal off some of the sources of supply. So the pushers have found another source — Mexico. It's not such good quality, but who's picky about these things? Not the pushers, or the addicts who're desperate for the stuff.

'It became obvious to us that the morphine produced in Mexico was being refined somewhere in the Caribbean and then exported to Florida, and after a lot of patient investigation we decided that Haiti was the place in question. It figures, doesn't it? The French Connection, Caribbean-style? But we still couldn't discover who was behind it or how it came into the States, not until the body of a man was found in Miami. He turned out to be a Guanian, and he was also a pusher on a small scale. This made us look at this island a bit more carefully, and what we found made us believe that the key to the whole operation is here. I was sent down to kind of merge into the scenery and do a preliminary investigation.'

'And Nick? Where does he come into it?'

'I asked for assistance — it was an impossible job on my own, but being a British Colony it was decided that it would be more diplomatic if someone British were sent down. I was real mad at the time. I wanted Hank Muller to come, a guy I've worked with for years, but instead I got this Limey flyer!'

'I still don't understand. Why Nick?'

'He had to have a valid reason for being on the island. Guani Group Airlines were looking for a pilot, so the top brass decided to ask for a Brit who could also fly. Nick had evidently distinguished himself in some security deal in Washington and was on the spot to be rushed to Miami for briefing in a hurry, so he was assigned here, for as long as it takes. But only very unofficially. The RAF didn't want to know about it. They've put him on indefinite sick leave, or some deal like that.'

'So he hasn't resigned from the RAF?'

'He hasn't resigned, and he hasn't dropped out. I'm sure your father will be delighted to know that. There's just this small problem of locating him.' He was silent for a moment. 'Just for the record,' he went on, 'he's one helluva guy. I stopped regretting Hank Muller months ago.'

'I'm glad of that. But Tom, where *is* he?'

'I don't know — I really don't know. He could have seen something, gone after someone; or someone could have gone after him, I guess. I hadn't thought anyone was on to us.'

'Are you on to anyone?'

He sighed.

'Now you know so much, I guess you might as well hear the lot. We're ninety nine point nine percent certain that Tony da Costa is the big guy — the brains behind the whole thing, and he's the one we're out to get. But there's no proof. Nothing that could stand up in a court of law. That's why Donna was assigned to him. We hoped she'd rake up something in the way of evidence, but so far, no dice. Lew Shroeder is part of it, but he's a lot lower on the totem pole. I think Betty's aware of it, poor woman. That's why she's in such a neurotic state. We thought at one time that Phil Prophet was one of the gang, but we made a mistake there.'

'Is that why Nick — '

'Sure. Stella took a shine for him right from the beginning, so he played along to see what he could find out. Phil isn't above smuggling the odd quantity of grass — every trip he makes to Haiti, he brings back some for Stella, but it's strictly for domestic consumption. We're sure now that he has nothing to do with this big operation.'

'So Stella's on pot. That explains a lot.'

'She has her problems. Don't judge her too harshly.'

'How did you get on to Lew?'

'A lot of patient toil. He lied about the hotel. He said one night that he'd bought it with money left to him by his father — a superfluous piece of information that no one asked for. But we checked it out — just then we were checking on everything that anyone said, and we got the word back that his dear old dad had died bankrupt in a home for alcoholics. So wherever Lew had gotten the money it wasn't from him. Before he came here, he was managing a hotel in Haiti — managing it, you notice, not owning it. So how did he manage to raise the $50,000 necessary to buy the Guani Inn? It was almost all in cash too. No mortgage. Seemed just like he must have had a money tree in his back yard.'

'And what was the connection with Tony da Costa?'

'The boys back in Florida sifted through all the information we gave them on everyone of any substance in the island — that was when we were thankful the population was no larger — and from the mug shots and fingerprints we were able to send them we established that da Costa had a police record and at one time was known to be connected with the Mafia. He did time about fifteen years ago for pushing drugs — and guess who was in the same section of the same prison at the same time? Lew Shroeder. Now I know it's a small world, but it seems a little more

121

than mere coincidence that they find themselves on the same little Caribbean island, doesn't it?'

I closed my eyes.

'I must be dreaming,' I said faintly. 'I find this all utterly unbelievable.' I opened my eyes again and glared at him fiercely. 'You're not putting me on, are you? You really are serious this time?'

'Lady, I was never more so. This is for real and Nick is missing for real, and what in hell's name I'm to do about it, I don't know.'

'Should we tell the police?'

'In the person of Major Williamson?' Tom shook his head. 'I guess we may have to eventually, but it'll be a last resort. He'd be as much use as an umbrella in a hurricane.'

'He knows about you, of course.'

'Oh, sure — but we avoid him as far as possible. We make the odd report to him, just to keep him in touch, but oh brother, his methods went out twenty-five years ago, at a modest estimate. Can you imagine anything more plain stupid than hauling you into the station and advising you to leave? We *told* him we'd see to it, but oh no, he had to put in his ten cents' worth. We went to pay a call on him the night you arrived, so he knew the way we felt about it.'

'So that's where you'd been: I saw you

122

coming back.' It seemed ages ago, that first night on the beach. Another world. 'Tom, would Donna know anything about Nick?'

'I doubt it. Anyway, I daren't contact her at the house. Da Costa is always there and there are too many extension telephones. There's a boy-friend of da Costa's there too, who's always prowling around.'

'A boy-friend?'

'Sure — he's as bent as a corkscrew.'

'But everyone seems to think that Donna . . . '

'Window dressing. He likes to have a pretty girl around to give a sort of normal image to the set-up. Borelli is supposed to be a handyman-chauffeur, and most people accept him as such. It's just that we've had the guy under a pretty powerful microscope these last few months. Believe me, he's my least favourite character in fact or fiction. I only wish we could turn up some real evidence against him.'

'He seems to enjoy his ill-gotten gains. Donna pointed out his boat to me yesterday.'

'Great, isn't it? When I think of the crummy thing I'm supposed to operate my business with! The Florida Police sure went to great trouble to make me look like an impoverished, third-rate diver. And if those spares don't come, I'll be a diver without a boat, any moment now. It may be good cover, but — '

He broke off sharply as the sound of a car, it's exhaust system long since rusted away, chugged laboriously to a halt outside the cottage.

'That's Nick,' he said, and was at the door in one bound.

'Thank God!' I breathed, coming up behind him and peering out. 'But just look at him, Tom. What on earth has happened?'

6

'Easy!' Tom said quietly. 'Save the screams of delight until he's safely behind closed doors. In fact, I should go and put the coffee on again, if I were you.'

I went swiftly to the kitchen and filled the percolator again. I also put a kettle on to boil and went to the cupboard in the tiny shower room to hunt for some disinfectant. From the look on Nick's blood-caked face, there was some swift first aid to be done.

By the time I returned to the living room, Nick was inside and had subsided wearily into a chair. He was soaking wet, but seemingly too exhausted to be conscious of it.

'Get you something?' Tom asked. 'There's coffee.'

'I'd rather have Scotch.'

Tom poured the drink and handed it to him.

'You'd better get out of those wet clothes,' I said.

Nick appeared to notice my presence for the first time.

'What the hell are you doing here?' he asked.

'I couldn't leave without knowing what had happened to you,' I said, coming closer to him. 'Nick, let me do something about your face.'

He waved me aside impatiently.

'Tom, you should have made her go.'

'Yeah? Me and whose army?' Tom enquired. He gave Nick a few more moments respite. 'Feel ready to talk?' he said at last.

Nick looked at me and said nothing.

'Don't mind me,' I told him. 'Tom told me everything.'

'It seemed pointless holding out any longer,' Tom said. 'She's involved now, whether she likes it or not. Whether we like it or not.'

'She should have gone,' Nick said again. But there was no heat in his voice. He seemed too weary to be much concerned one way or the other.

'What happened, Nick?'

Nick took a long swallow of his drink.

'You're not going to like this, mate. I feel all kinds of a fool.'

'Go on,' Tom said, without expression.

'I was on my way back,' Nick began at last, 'waiting for clearance to land. There was some light plane taking off, so I had to circle. I had no passengers for the return flight. There was a load of tourists going over to

126

West Guani, but coming back I was on my own, so just for the hell of it I took a wider sweep than usual and flew over da Costa's house. Right out of the usual flight path, as you know. No one could have expected me.'

'So?'

'I saw something that made me think this was the break we'd been looking for. There was a man, half-way up the cliff below the house.'

'But that's a sheer drop!'

'That's what made me look twice. I couldn't see how anyone could have climbed up or down to that point. So I kept looking — and he disappeared, Tom, right before my very eyes. Now you see him, now you don't sort of thing.'

'A cave?'

'That's what I thought immediately.'

'So you went to see? On your own? Without waiting to tell me where you'd gone?' Tom's voice was hard.

'Look, I know it seems crazy in the light of what happened but you weren't around, Tom. You were diving, remember? I didn't have any intention of investigating it properly, but I wanted to mark the place while it was fresh in my mind. I thought it would take me ten minutes at the most to get there, perhaps another fifteen to snoop around a little, and I could be back at the hotel to see Liz before she'd even noticed I was late.'

'So what went wrong?' Tom sounded exasperated but at the same time, resigned.

'Give me another Scotch, will you?' Nick held out his glass and I leapt to refill it.

'I drove to Crescent Beach from the Airport and climbed over the rocks to just below where he'd been standing and I managed to get up to it. Don't ask me how! When I came to climb down again, I nearly killed myself.'

'Go on,' Tom said grimly.

'Once I'd made the ledge it wasn't too bad. I inched along it to where I thought I'd seen the guy, and sure enough, there was a cave opening. I thought it was just a shallow cleft at first. It was hardly big enough to squeeze through, but once inside it opened out into a tunnel of sorts.'

'That's when you should have come away.'

'You don't have to tell me! I'm sorry, Tom — but you know how it is. I kept thinking that if I went another few yards, I'd find something. I can't deny it, it was sheer curiosity that kept me going. I had a little pocket torch I'd taken from the car, but the batteries were on the blink and it didn't give much light. After a bit, though, I realized that the light was getting better. At first I thought

I was coming out on the cliff again somewhere — the tunnel twisted round quite a lot, and I got a bit confused about the direction — but then I saw that the light was artificial. Then I knew I was on to something, Tom! I couldn't stop then!'

'Where was this light? I don't quite get the picture.'

'At the end of the tunnel where it widened out into an underground cave.'

'Anything there?'

'Nothing that I could see — well, just a few stalactites and stalagmites and quite a lot of water, but nothing incriminating. But the tunnel seemed to continue over the other side of the cave. There were intermittent lights all the way along in the roof of the tunnel behind metal cage things, so I just followed my nose and after a while I thought I heard voices. I went on and finally the tunnel stopped. The voices were obviously pretty near by this time, so I decided discretion was the better part and ducked down behind a convenient rock, where I could see.'

'See what?'

'There was a cave in front of me — a deep cave, full of water. And there was a boat moored there, Tom, that makes da Costa's cruiser outside the hotel look like a paddle-boat in a pleasure park. A brand new Sea Ray with a 250 h.p. inboard. Da Costa and Borelli were on board, messing about with the engine, but only for a few minutes. Then they went up some steps to a tunnel on the far side of the cave, switched off the lights and disappared.

'Did you hear anything useful?'

'They were discussing the latest ball game between the Miami Dolphins and some team from Jacksonville. Not a word about the junk.'

'So then you came straight back like a good boy?'

'Well,' Nick said, a little sheepishly, 'not exactly. I thought I'd try to find the light switch and have a look around the Sea Ray. It was pitch dark, but I managed to swim across the cave and find the steps, and it was fairly easy to feel my way to the switch. I'm telling you, man, that boat was really something! Every latest fishing gadget you can imagine. Two berths and the neatest galley you ever saw — and white wall to wall carpeting in the saloon!'

'Any junk?'

'Not a sign. I really pulled it apart — discreetly, of course. But there was no trace.'

'Any place where it could be?'

'I imagine there must be. After all, even a million dollars' worth of snow doesn't take up that much amount of room. One place I thought was a distinct possibility was underneath the carpet. It was very thick — kind of cushiony, if you know what I mean, with a rubber backing. It struck me that if the junk was in small packets it might well go between the pile and the backing.'

'Wall to wall snow!' Tom whistled. 'It's a thought. The whole thing sounds the sort of craft you can see around Miami or Fort Lauderdale any day of the week. But I don't get it, Nick. How the hell do they figure on getting it out of the cave?'

'Sorry, I forgot that bit. There are massive steel doors on the seaward side.'

'Steel doors? But how the hell haven't we noticed that from the outside? We've sailed round there often enough.'

'Think, Tom. I was able to climb up to the ledge — just — but I'd never have been able to go on. The cliff is absolutely sheer directly underneath da Costa's house, and there are loads of coral heads just under the sea surface — right? If the gates were camouflaged sufficiently well, no one would ever go near enough to spot the difference. You know yourself we always keep well out at that point.'

131

'That's true. But what a feat of engineering!'

'That's why he brought down builders from the States!' I chipped in.

Both their heads swung around to look at me. They had obviously forgotten my existence.

'So he did,' Tom said. 'That figures. But we have to find the snow! You can't convict a man for keeping a luxury boat in a cave that happens to be under his house.'

'Nick, I wish you'd let me do something about your face,' I said anxiously. 'What happened?'

'Well,' he said, 'after I'd had a good look round the boat, I went up the tunnel again and switched the lights out, and somehow, in the darkness, I — I managed to get lost. I just plain lost my bloody way! Those caves stretch for miles, I'm telling you! They must be part of the same system as those on the south point, or another just like it. Anyway, I blundered around for what seemed hours — well, it *was* hours! — and had just about resigned myself to being buried alive, when I came across the ledge where I'd left my torch. Believe me, I've never been more relieved in the whole of my life! After that it was easy — except for the climb down. If we ever do it again, we'll have to take a rope. It's foolhardy to attempt it without.'

'*Now* he says it! Man, the whole deal was foolhardy. Did it occur to you that you could have been seen? If you ever do anything like that again, I'll get you taken off the case, so help me God! Meanwhile, go clean your face. You don't want coral poisoning.'

'Damn right I don't.' Nick rose from his chair. 'Liz, rustle me up some food while I have a shower, will you? I'm starving.' He stood looking hesitantly at Tom.

'I'm willing to bet you would have done the same,' he said.

'I,' said Tom coldly, 'would not have gotten myself lost. Hey,' he added, as Nick mooched off, deflated, to the bathroom. 'Where did you leave your car? I went up and down the road to Crescent Beach twice.'

A little of Nick's bounce returned, and he laughed.

'And you didn't find it? Well, that was the idea. I didn't want anyone to know I was snooping.'

'But where was it?'

'In a place where it looked so natural you wouldn't even notice it. I drove it into the car graveyard, right between an old Chevvy with no innards and a VW resting on its back axle. There were a couple of tyres lying on the ground, so I opened the nearside door and hung one of them over it and shoved some twisted metal on the roof — believe me, my poor old jalopy looked as disreputable as any of them.'

'You were lucky to find it still had an engine when you got back to it,' Tom said. But he looked amused and I was hopeful that the worst of his annoyance with Nick had been dissipated.

'I've just realized,' I said later, after we had eaten and were sitting over coffee, 'that I haven't told the hotel I shall be there tonight after all. Though I imagine they must know I wasn't on the plane.'

'I told them,' Tom said, 'while you were busy patching up Our Hero.'

'Get knotted,' Nick said pleasantly.

'What reason did you give?' I asked.

'Oh, I said we'd managed to make you change your mind. It was difficult, I said, but we finally made it. Say, what's all this about going to Haiti? Ellen Myers heard me talking to Betty and started yakking about how lovely it was, now you can go with them after all.'

'So I could! She mentioned it on the beach yesterday. You're taking them, aren't you, Nick? Ellen said there would be a spare seat, and why didn't I go along too. What do you think of the idea? I gather they'll be back on Sunday.'

'Sounds like a great idea.'

'I thought you might think so. At least it gets me out of the way!'

'You'll enjoy it.'

'A thought strikes me.' Nick was obviously tired out from the events of this day, but roused himself sufficiently to speak. 'Why don't you come to Haiti with us and fly back to London from there? That way you won't have to wait until Tuesday's plane.'

'Oh Nick! Do I have to?'

'I wish you would. Can't you see there's enough for us to worry about without being concerned for your safety?'

'What makes you think this thing is about to blow up before Tuesday? Surely I can wait until then?'

'We have the word from Florida,' Tom explained. 'The Narcotics Bureau always know when a big shipment is due. They've had the known peddlers under surveillance for weeks, and by their behaviour it's obvious that something big is about to break. We're fighting against time.'

'Somehow we have to nail da Costa with the goods,' Nick added. 'We know he's the Mr Big we're looking for, but he's a crafty bastard — somehow he always manages to keep his hands clean. I'm willing to bet that if and when that beautiful boat sails for Florida,

Tony da Costa will be at dinner in Government House or in church, or somewhere. But the fact remains that something is going to happen very soon Liz, and we want you out.'

I sighed, but was resigned.

'I suppose I'll have to do as you say. But under strong protest! I want to know what happens.'

'I'll drop you a postcard,' Nick said, and yawned. 'Meanwhile, I'm off to bed.'

Left alone, Tom and I looked at each other.

'Well,' Tom said. 'Quite a day, one way and another.'

'You could say so. Do I really have to go, Tom?'

'Yes.'

There really wasn't much use in arguing with that. I shrugged.

'Oh well, I've had a two day reprieve — and it's given me a chance to see Haiti.

'And tomorrow there's da Costa's party. We'll go and have us a ball.'

'We will? Tom, you amaze me! I shouldn't have thought you'd want to go.'

'And be conspicuous by our absence? You forget that this is an island where everyone's actions are under a microscope. Nicky and I are two fun-loving, swinging bachelors. We wouldn't dare miss it.'

'But what about me? I'm not invited.'

'That doesn't matter. Nor will half of the guests there be invited. No, you must come with us — it would be the most natural thing.'

'Anything you say,' I said lightly.

'Anything? How about a walk on the beach?'

'I — I don't think so, Tom.' I spoke hesitantly. 'I'm pretty tired myself. I think I'll go to bed too.' I got to my feet and looked at him. 'Besides — ' I said, and stopped.

He came over to me and held my elbows in his two hands.

'Besides what, honey?'

I sighed and rested my head against his shoulder.

'I don't know, Tom. I just think it would be better if I went straight to bed. Last night was . . .'

'Last night was pretty wonderful, I thought.'

'It was disturbing.'

'So what's wrong with that?'

'I don't know,' I said again. 'I find it hard to put my feelings into words.'

'You don't want to get involved, is that it?'

'Nor do you, Tom!'

His arms slid round me.

'Not right now, maybe. But there are other

times and other places. And I *was* only suggesting a walk on the beach.'

'I know. But I don't think so, Tom. Not tonight.'

He stood looking down at me.

'I know the trouble with you,' he said. 'That creep from Miami has made you anti-American.'

'Nonsense! I'm not an-*tie* anyone,' I said, mimicking his accent. 'Least of all you. But I'm tired and confused and I want to go to bed.'

'Say, that's not such a bad idea!' He reached for me again, but I evaded him neatly.

'You may walk me home,' I said, laughing at him.

'Huh! Big deal! Do I get to dance with you at the party tomorrow, too?'

'If you ask nicely.'

'Oh, I'll ask *reeeal* nice — and we can dance under the stars and try to forget that, once again, it's your last night here. Come on, you ice-cold little Limey.'

He walked me back to the hotel, his arm around my shoulders, and in spite of his kiss — quite as disturbing as those of the night before — I slept soundly and dreamlessly.

7

The group in the corner, dressed in white frilled satin shirts and red flared trousers, belted out pop-music with more enthusiasm than skill, but no one minded.

The patio, jutting out over the silvery sea, the darker humps of the small off-shore islands just visible, was ringed with coloured lights. A bar with a striped awning was set up in another corner, and the entire population of the island — or so it seemed to me — was there, talking, laughing, drinking and dancing. Beautiful black girls, beautiful coffee-coloured girls, and beautiful white girls; what a lot of beautiful people, I thought — or was it the result of that harmless-tasting rum punch that had been handed to me on arrival? A beautiful young man handed me another, and not until he had left me did I realize that it was Jimmy. It had to be the effect of the rum, I decided. I had not considered him particularly beautiful in the cold light of day.

It was a night that seemed made for enjoyment, and the islanders of all colours were demonstrating enthusiastically that they had an unbounded capacity for it. I only wished that I could be as carefree as the rest of them. On the way to the house Tom had told me that when the party was in full swing he was going to look round the house.

'Da Costa should be fully occupied with his guests,' he said, 'and I guess Borelli will be behind the bar.'

'Aren't there any other servants?'

'Yes, there are two girls — but my guess is they'll be acting as waitresses. You and Nick will have to see everyone stays away.'

'That could be difficult.'

'I'll wait until after supper — I believe there's usually a buffet, and clearing it away should keep the maids busy. Just relax and be natural. You're going there to enjoy yourself.'

How I wished that was true! It would have been easy to forget the darker side of the island for once, in the whirl of music and laughter that was going on all around me. I would have been glad to unwind among innocent people who, ignorant of the despicable traffic being carried under their noses, were simply out for an evening's enjoyment. I forced myself to stop looking around to check Tom's whereabouts and concentrated on dancing with Nick.

He had taken me over to meet Tony da

Costa as soon as we arrived. Not unnaturally, I was curious to meet this, by now, almost legendary figure, and felt some surprise that he looked so ordinary. Not that I expected horns and a tail, exactly, but such a mild-mannered gentleman came as a surprise. He was above average height and of slim build. His dark hair was receding, but showed no sign of grey although I judged that he must be between forty-five and fifty. He was a good-looking man with a flashing smile, a white polo-necked silk shirt, and a very large cigar.

'I'm afraid I'm gate-crashing,' I said, after Nick had introduced me. 'My brother insisted that you wouldn't mind.'

'I wish all gate-crashers were as pretty as you,' he said. 'My house is yours.'

We exchanged pleasantries until other guests claimed his attention and Nick led me on to the dance floor.

'He doesn't seem a bad sort,' I said.

'Appearances,' said Nick, 'are deceptive. Oh God, there's Stella! She looks as if she's smashed out of her tiny mind already.'

Stella had caught sight of us and was waving wildly to Nick, who forced himself to smile and wave back. She swooped down upon us at the same time as a tall, gangling islander cut in on me, and Nick and I were swept apart. Loosen up, Jimmy had advised me. Did he have this in mind, I wondered? Just how loose could anyone get? My partner seemed to have bones made of rubber and rhythm pulsating in his blood. It was impossible to converse. We just smiled happily at each other from time to time and went on dancing.

There was no shortage of partners. I danced with a young Government surveyor, red faced with his exertions and slightly off the beat; a sharp-featured schoolmaster, far from academic in purple flares and a flowered shirt; a local bank clerk with an Afro hair-style and a spotted bow-tie; and Jimmy, who was actually wearing a clean T-shirt for the occasion.

Finally I begged him for a rest.

'Jimmy, I'm exhausted! I must sit down and have a drink.'

'OK love, I'll get you one.'

He left me sitting on the wall which bordered the patio, and taking advantage of the lull, I looked around for Tom. He was over by the bar, talking to a girl in a red dress. I might have preferred him to be talking to me, but at least I didn't have to worry about his whereabouts — not just then. Stella was clinging to Nick in a way that made dancing all but impossible. Donna was standing in a group with Tony da Costa and an older couple, looking flatteringly attentive to her boss.

When Jimmy came over with my drink, he was trailing a girl behind him — a beautiful, brown-skinned girl, dazzlingly dressed in a silver and white gown, clinging to her superb figure as if it had been pasted on.

It took me a minute to recognize her.

'Why, Araminta!' I said at last. 'You look gorgeous!'

The girl hung her head, biting her lip. I imagined that she was feeling shy, but Jimmy propelled her forward, apparently without regard for her feelings.

'Come on, Minta,' he said. 'What've you got to say to Miss Marshall?'

Still the girl hung back, saying nothing and looking close to tears.

'Stop being such a bully,' I said to Jimmy. 'Come on, Araminta. Come and sit next to me for a bit.'

Araminta shook her head mutely, refusing to look at me. Jimmy gave her a push.

'Minta, you promised,' he said sternly.

The girl looked at him appealingly, wringing her hands, but his expression was implacable. Seeing no hope there, she finally looked me in the face.

'I — I have to say I'm sorry, ma'am,' she

said at last, in a voice so low that it was scarcely audible.

'Sorry? What for?'

'For the crab.'

'For the — you mean it was *you*? But why?'

Araminta seemed to gather the remnants of her dignity around her and lifted her head proudly.

'I wanted to frighten you, ma'am. I wanted you to leave the hotel.'

I looked at her in bewilderment.

'But why, Araminta?' I asked again.

The girl hesitated, but at a nudge from Jimmy she spoke.

'It was because of him,' she said, indicating Jimmy with a lift of her chin. 'I thought — I thought — '

'She thought I was making a pass at you,' Jimmy explained. 'Remember? I came and sat down beside you and sort of chatted you up a bit. The silly girl jumped to conclusions.'

I leaned back against the wall and laughed.

'What's so damn funny?' Jimmy asked in an injured tone. 'After all, you could have taken a fancy to me, couldn't you? It's not outside the realms of possibility.'

'It's just the relief,' I explained hastily. 'It all seemed so sinister. Somehow this explanation never entered my head.'

'Well, anyway,' Jimmy said, 'she's sorry, aren't you, Minta?'

Araminta nodded.

'And you'll never do such a silly thing again?'

She shook her head violently.

I reached out a hand to her.

'Come and sit down with me, Araminta,' I said. 'Go away, Jimmy. This is woman to woman.'

He left us and headed to the bar, while Araminta hesitantly sat on the wall beside me. There was silence between us for a moment.

'You really love him, don't you?' I said at last.

She nodded. 'Yes ma'am, I sure do.'

'I like him too — oh, not in the way you do, just as a friend, you understand. Somehow he seems very young to me.'

'He's not so young.'

'Oh, I know he's not. I mean in the way he behaves — the way he thinks.'

Araminta nodded again.

'Sure, ma'am, I knows what you means. But all men is wild like boys. That's how come they need a woman.'

I looked at the girl and smiled. Maybe she was right. Maybe she was the very girl for Jimmy. Most English girls would expect too much of him. Araminta accepted him the way he was. Suddenly I felt ashamed. I'd had some idea in my mind of the necessity to warn Araminta of Jimmy's defects in character, but now I knew that she recognized them and loved him just the same. Maybe there's a lesson there for you, Liz Marshall, I thought to myself.

'How did you get that crab in the wardrobe?' I asked her.

'I was just going home,' she explained, 'when I seen you go down the steps and on to the beach. And then I seen the crab. Man, he was awful big. I don't never see a crab so big before.'

'I know!' I shuddered at the memory.

'I scooped it up in my shopping bag and ran up the steps to your room, and put it in your closet. Guess you never seen me!'

'No, I didn't. And I was very frightened.'

'I'm real sorry, ma'am. I knows I was wrong about you and Jimmy — but it was only an old crab! 'Twouldn't have done no harm.'

'It just scared me half to death, that's all. Well, never mind now — that's all over and forgotten.'

'And you won't tell Mrs Schroeder?'

'Not if you promise never to do such a thing again.'

'I never will, ma'am. Honest to God.'

'How about a dance, Liz?'

I looked up and saw Tom standing before me.

'One mystery solved,' I told him as we drifted away together in a slow number. 'Araminta planted the crab.'

'It figures,' he said, after I had explained. 'That sort of thing would be a natural reaction. If she'd actually caught you in the act, she would have burnt your house down.'

'I find her devotion rather touching.'

'Misplaced, to say the least.'

'You have no romance in your nature,' I told him.

'You'd better believe it,' he said. But he held me close, and the feel of his lips against my temple made me breathless.

We drew apart reluctantly when the music finished and stood looking at each other for a moment without speaking. He reached out a finger and touched my cheek.

'Liz? we'll meet again, won't we? When all this is over.'

I hesitated.

'I don't know, Tom. Will we?'

'I think we have to.'

His expression was serious, but even as he looked at me, he began to smile — a wide, false smile.

'Tony da Costa is coming over,' he said, continuing to stroke my cheek. 'I think I'll go and explore right now. Keep him talking.'

'I came to ask my delightful visitor from London to dance,' da Costa said. 'May I?'

'Of course,' I said. 'Excuse me, Tom.'

Tom drifted off into the crowd that surrounded the patio, as I went into da Costa's arms. He danced well, in a rather old-fashioned sort of way, and I complimented him.

'I was on the stage once,' he told me. 'Many years ago. Dancing was a necessary part of the training.'

'And now I believe you're a collector of beautiful things.'

'That's right. I must show you my treasures some time.'

'I should love to see them.'

Now that he mentioned it, I could tell that his rather precise diction was stagey. We talked about the theatre and actors in general, and then he progressed to a certain actor in particular and told me a horrendously scurrilous piece of scandal. In my experience, men just didn't *do* things like that — and I remembered Tom's assertion that the man was 'bent as a corkscrew'. I felt inclined to believe him.

The music stopped. There was still no sign

of Tom and I knew that I had to stick with da Costa somehow. I asked him for a drink, and we went over to the bar together. Nick was already there with Donna and Stella, and as he turned to speak to us, I gave him a meaningful glance, which I hoped he interpreted as a signal that Tom was off on his exploratory mission.

How we talked to da Costa! We flattered him and laughed at his jokes. I questioned him about his collection of coins and professed myself ignorant, but interested to the point of obsession. Nick admired his house and his boat and his private plane, and his skill at the controls. Donna told us all what a marvellous boss he was and how she loved working for him. And da Costa stood there modestly, flicking ash from his cigar and lapping it all up, like a cat with a saucer of cream.

I had noticed Borelli behind the bar from the beginning of the evening. He was a thickset, stocky man, with dark, greasy hair, considerably younger than da Costa but far less elegant. He had served drinks non-stop, hardly talking to anyone — so much part of the furniture that one hardly registered the fact of his presence. Suddenly, in the middle of what had become our game with da Costa, I looked towards the bar and saw that his presence was a fact no longer. Borelli had gone, his place taken by one of the maids.

Nick was standing with his back to the bar.

'Ah,' I said gaily. 'A change of barman!'

He turned round slowly, registered Borelli's absence, and turned back again, without a change of expression. But as soon as there was a lull in the conversation he asked Donna to dance, and with a long look at me, disappeared with her into the throng.

So it was all up to me. I had to keep da Costa occupied on my own now, while he and Donna checked on Borelli's whereabouts. And like a bad actor, I dried completely.

What more could I talk about? I had, I felt, said all I could ever say on the subject of coins and stamps. We had admired the house ad nauseam. My brain was even devoid of comments on the theatre. But that, surely, was the key! Every actor likes to talk about himself.

'What was your favourite role?' I asked him.

Thank heaven, it seemed the right thing to say, and lasted us almost to the end of another drink.

'Let *me* get you another,' I cried hysterically, seizing his glass. 'After all, it is your birthday! And have you ever acted in

Britain? Or in Hollywood? On television, perhaps?'

I kept the questions coming thick and fast and was just about at the end of my tether by the time I felt a hand clutch mine, and turned round to see Tom.

'I've come to ask you to dance,' he said. 'If Tony will agree to part with you.'

I had the feeling that Tony was as relieved as I at my departure.

'Where have you *been*?' I hissed at Tom, smiling brightly. 'It's been a nightmare! I thought I was going to have to keep talking for ever.'

He laughed.

'You sure were going great guns when I came up. Your hands are like ice!'

'I was frightened, Tom! You were away so long, and Borelli disappeared too. Nick and Donna went to look for him and left me alone with that egotistical old matinée idol.'

'Old *what*?'

'Matinée idol! Didn't you know he used to be on the stage?'

Tom laughed again.

'I believe he did do a television commercial for Southern Comfort once. Is that the line he's been feeding you?'

I sagged against him.

'Thank heaven I didn't know that! I really

151

would have been at a loss for something to talk about. But was it worth it, Tom? Did you find out anything?'

'Only that da Costa is going to Miami tomorrow — flying himself in his own plane.'

'Who told you that?'

'Borelli. I met him in the john.'

'Is that where he went! He was gone a long time.'

'It was only a few minutes ago that I talked to him. He'd been packing da Costa's clothes and papers, ready for his flight tomorrow.'

'So you didn't have a chance to search?'

'I turned over the study while Borelli was busy upstairs. Nothing. But I don't want to talk about it here.'

The music stopped, and the band were preparing to take a rest. To cope with this emergency, da Costa had engaged the services of a local rip-saw band (a description of which I had managed to drag out for several minutes), and this more tatterdemalion crew were beginning to get into position.

'Here's where we sit down,' Tom said. 'There's no way I can dance to that!'

Suddenly there was a frenzied burst of drumming which made all heads turn towards the drummer. It was Jimmy, taking advantage of the drummer's absence to appropriate his drums, and he appeared to be in the grip of some sort of madness, bashing away at each of the drums in turn, clashing the cymbal, all with a maniacal smile on his face and the occasional shout of ecstasy.

At first the guests smiled and applauded, but the noise was so prolonged that people grew uneasy, especially as it became obvious that the drummer had given no permission for this take-over. He was standing on the edge of the platform silently expostulating — silent, because no voice could possibly be heard over the din. The rip-saw band were now ready with their saws and washboards and one-stringed fiddles, and they, too, became more and more agitated as Jimmy refused to give up the spotlight.

Tom looked grim.

'That cretin. There'll be an international incident if someone doesn't shut him up. That drummer is about to haul off and punch him in the nose.'

'Can't anyone stop him?'

'I will myself.'

Tom made as if to go over to the platform, but stopped in his tracks as the noise suddenly abated.

Araminta had gone up to the rostrum and had calmly wrested the drum-sticks from him. Smiling sweetly, she put boths arms round Jimmy's neck, saying something to the drummer and smiling at him over her shoulder in such a way that his anger evaporated. In a moment the rip-saw band had swung into their first number with its funny hop, skip and jump rhythm, and the incident was over.

'Neatly done,' Tom commented.

'Maybe she'll reform him yet.'

'I almost feel sorry for the guy. Look, Liz, would you mind very much if we split?'

'Split?'

'Blew. Got the hell out of here. My party spirit seems to have evaporated.'

'Anything you want. What about Nick?'

'Let's go and talk to him.'

We walked round the edge of the patio towards Nick, who had Stella draped over him once more. He greeted our arrival with obvious relief and immediately extricated himself in order to lead me on to the dance floor.

'Hadn't you better watch it?' I asked. 'It looks to me like a pistols-for-two-and-coffee-for-one situation.'

Nick sighed heavily.

'So help me, Liz, I'll never get into this sort of situation again. I only wish Phil would show a bit of animation — it's what Stella wants. She's a very lonely, unhappy woman.'

'Very heart-rending,' I commented wryly.

'But as far as you're concerned, she's bad news, as Tom would say.'

'All should resolve itself very shortly. Talking of Tom . . . ' he stopped and looked at me quizzically. 'Do you two have anything going? It sort of looks that way to me.'

I smiled at him sweetly.

'Wouldn't you like to know, little brother? By the way, he wants us to leave.'

'Us? Just you, or you and me?'

'Either, I imagine.'

'Then I'll stay if you don't mind — and something tells me you won't. I'm rather enjoying this false atmosphere of innocent enjoyment. By the way, Donna tells me that da Costa's going away tomorrow and leaving her behind. That's unusual.'

'Tom knows. Borelli told him.'

'I wonder what significance there is in that?'

I asked Tom what he thought about it when we were in the car and heading away from the house on the ridge.

'Do you think da Costa suspects her?' I asked. 'Nick seemed to think it strange that he's not taking her.'

'It's unusual, certainly. He goes all over the place on buying trips and she usually goes along too, but I don't think this necessarily means that he's on to her. I'd think it means

155

quite the reverse. He must think she's one of his usual dumb blonde broads who has no idea of what's going on. Otherwise he would hardly leave her alone here, with plenty of opportunity to snoop about.'

'Did Donna have any comments about the boat Nick discovered?'

'It was as much a surprise to her as to us. One thing — she's thought for a long time that there's something in da Costa's study hidden behind one of the bookcases. She thought it was a safe, but hasn't been able to find what activates the mechanism to move it. It seems likely now that it's not a safe at all, but the doors to the tunnel leading to the cave. She's going to try to investigate it this weekend.'

'I wish it were all over. What else do you need, Tom? Is it enough if she finds the heroin down there?'

'Enough to nail da Costa. But we still haven't anything on the Haitian angle. I'd love to clean that up too. So far we have no idea how the stuff gets here. Every sloop or plane from Haiti is torn apart, but we haven't found so much as a grain. I guess the field is even wider now that we've found the boat. They could rendezvous at sea just about anywhere to take the junk on board.'

'Aren't there any coastguards?'

'Honey, have you worked out the proportion of sea to land in these parts? There is one Police launch, but that's fully occupied chasing lobster poachers. No — they've got the whole wide ocean to operate in. We'd need a hot line to God to find out where the delivery takes place.'

'Where are you going?' I asked, seeing that we were keeping on the coast road and not turning towards the cluster of lights that marked the little town.

'Somewhere quiet and peaceful. Right to the south point, where there's nothing but sandpipers and herons and fish eagles.'

He pulled off the track on to a rocky plateau overlooking the gently tossing sea, and in the silence as he switched off the engine, we could hear the murmurous surf and the sudden cry of the night bird.

We got out of the car and leaned against it, side by side, welcoming the soft, moist breeze.

'This is getting to be quite a habit, isn't it? Spending your last nights with me, I mean.'

'Mm. Only this really is the last night.'

'Will you be staying in Haiti, or going straight on?'

'I haven't made up my mind. I'll see how I feel.'

'I wish I could show you around. There's a

lovely French restaurant I know where the escargots are out of this world.' He was silent for a few moments, but I knew he was looking at me. 'Do you realize,' he said at last, 'that we haven't done one really fun thing since we met? We haven't gone sailing or swimming; I haven't taken you out to dinner or a movie. Even the party tonight was strictly business! It's just my luck to meet a girl like you when I'm so — preoccupied!'

'As you said, there are other times and places.'

'Is that a promise, Liz? There's a vacation due to me soon. I'll come to London in November.'

'It'll be cold in November,' I said inanely, as he turned my face towards his.

'We'll warm it up!'

His lips and hands and the closeness of his body were already creating a fire inside of me.

'Deal?' he asked, as he finally drew away.

'Deal,' I agreed shakily.

8

I think I would have found Port-au-Prince overwhelming at any time, but coming so quickly after the leisurely pace of Grand Guani the effect was mind-blowing. I was glad, as we drove from the Claude Duvalier airport, that we were insulated from the tangle of screeching, blaring traffic and the crowded pavements. An air-conditioned limousine from George's hotel had met us, and we sat in cushioned comfort, looking out at the confusion all around us.

But it was enchanting, too — the ride from the airport between flowering oleander bushes, the gaily decorated buses with their fanciful names and passengers clinging to every square inch; even the street hawkers and beggars added to the atmosphere.

The hotel was in the suburb of Petionville, away from the picturesque squalor that was Port-au-Prince, and as we climbed up from the town I was intrigued to see how the architecture of the houses remained so typically French, even in this Caribbean setting.

'Oh, I *am* glad I came,' I said to Ellen. 'I

can't thank you enough for thinking of it.'

We had left Grand Guani at what had appeared the crack of dawn and was, in fact, about half past eight — and now, three hours later, Ellen and I were stretched out by the swimming pool. George had left immediately for his business meeting, and Nick, too, had disappeared, having explained quietly to me that he was going to confer with Their Man in Haiti. He had offered to take me with him, but a combination of laziness and a feeling of obligation to Ellen, had made me refuse. Little did I know how later events would make me regret that decision!

They both returned at lunchtime and we all had a swim. After our pool-side lunch, Nick and I intended to see the sights. George had more business to attend to, and although we pressed Ellen to come with us, she protested that it was far too hot and that anyway, she had seen it all before.

'But maybe we could go shopping, Liz, if you come back in time? I want to buy an embroidered blouse for a niece of mine, and I'd like your advice. Then maybe we could dine at Chez Solange?' Ellen looked suddenly hesitant. 'Unless, of course, you have other plans.'

I had been hoping for a tête-a-tête with Nick now that relations between us were so much less strained, but I noticed the hesitation and realized Ellen's loneliness.

'We'd love to, wouldn't we Nick?'

'Sounds wonderful! Isn't that the place that's famous for its escargots?'

'That's it — and it's so beautiful! Set in a lovely garden, with such a wonderfully intimate atmosphere.'

Oh Tom, I thought, where art thou?

After lunch we found a taxi that was prepared to stay with us all afternoon and drove off towards Kenscoff, where small clouds blanketed the top of the mountains. The restored camaraderie between us gave our sight-seeing an added dimension and I was grateful for this interlude away from the tensions of Grand Guani. Nick seemed to put away all his preoccupations, and I felt as if I was rediscovering him after a lapse of years. We found much to laugh at and much to talk about — though after sampling the sixteen different types of rum at Jane Babancourt's Castle, I had the distinct impression that much of what was said was sheer nonsense. But what did it matter? Communication had been restored between us, and that made me happier than I had been for a long time.

Dinner at Chez Solange was perfection — gourmet food, beautifully served in opulent and unusual surroundings, and Ellen and George were delightful hosts. George was in an expansive mood, his business meeting having gone to his satisfaction. But both of them pleaded tiredness and the evening ended early.

'So now what?' Nick asked me, when the Myers had retired to bed and we were having our last nightcap together under the stars. 'Are you going back tomorrow?'

'I think so,' I said. 'It would seem an awful anticlimax to stay on my own. I'll come to the airport with you and see what's leaving for Miami.'

'There's bound to be something,' Nick agreed.

'I still hate going,' I said. 'In spite of everything, I'm glad I came.'

'Tom?'

'Well, partly. Nick, I don't *know* about Tom! Oh, I'm attracted to him, I'll admit that, but — but, I've made so many mistakes! I'm sort of distrustful of my own feelings, as well as in the dark about his.'

'He's your sort of person, Liz.'

'Maybe. Time will tell. But never mind about me — is this thing with Donna serious?'

'How do you know about it?' He sounded mystified. I hesitated, not wanting to

162

embarrass him by telling him what I had overheard.

'Oh — women's intuition, perhaps.'

'Huh!' Nick sounded sceptical. 'But to answer your question, I've never been more serious in my life. She's my girl, Liz. We're going to be married as soon as we get out of this mess.'

'Dad will be delighted!'

'You reckon? He won't mind that she's not True Blue British?'

'He'll regard her as a steadying influence. I hope 'this mess' is all over soon, Nick. I shan't have a moment's peace until I hear from you.'

'It can't be long,' he said. 'It *can't* be long.'

As I waved the little plane goodbye at the airport the following morning, his words echoed in my mind and I prayed that they were well-founded. The sight of the small aircraft winging away made me feel unexpectedly forlorn and alone, and I watched the diminishing dot until it disappeared from view. I was glad I had made the decision to leave Haiti that day.

I had put my case and hand luggage in a locker as it seemed likely that I would have a few hours to spare and I wanted to be free to look at the handicraft shops that operated in the airport building. At the last moment I had extracted my camera and taken a picture of Nick, Ellen and George, standing by the Islander before they took off, so that I was only lightly encumbered as — having checked that the next plane for Miami was a PanAm flight leaving in two and a half hours — I wandered out to the front of the departure lounge to see what was going on.

It was a moderately busy airport. A harassed tour operator was trying to round up his flock and seemed to be having trouble. Evidently the number of passports in his hand was greater than the total of passengers.

'Where is my lady?' he was bleating unhappily. 'Has anyone seen my lady?'

Nobody had, and my heart bled for him.

An Air France Caravelle taxied in on one runway, while a smaller jet destined for Jamaica was loading closer to the terminal. There were light planes in plenty. Aircraft recognition is hardly my forte — one small plane looks awfully like another to me, yet there looked something very familiar about the one that was coming in to land. A Beechcraft, I said to myself, feeling rather superior. Hadn't Nick pointed out its identical twin to me only yesterday morning, when we had left Grand Guani? Yes, it was quite definitely a Beechcraft — exactly like the one owned by Tony da Costa, the plane in which he was flying to Miami.

It came to rest and the propellers died. Sheer idle curiosity kept me there. I had absolutely no presentiment that down from the pilot's seat would jump Tony da Costa himself.

I stepped back quickly from the outside terrace into the shadows of the departure lounge. A figure was already striding across the tarmac to greet da Costa, and they walked back towards the buildings, engrossed in conversation.

His companion was tall. He topped da Costa by several inches, and had dark hair, crisp and Italianate, immaculately styled. He was a younger man with a thin moustache and restrained, expensive clothes. Together they made an elegant couple.

For a moment I thought they were heading for the normal entry to the airport, in which case I felt they could hardly fail to see me. I retreated even further into a corner, prepared to turn my back, but was intrigued to see that they appeared to be by-passing the normal immigration formalities. They had veered away from thc gatc carmarked for arriving passengers and had disappeared between two buildings, down a passageway which I guessed would lead directly to the outside concourse.

I remembered our own arrival. Immigration and customs had been particularly thorough. What was so different about Tony da Costa? The position and influence — and perhaps the readiness with cash — of his companion, was one answer that occurred to me.

I stood irresolutely for a moment. Why, oh why hadn't Tony da Costa arrived while Nick was still here? His appearance, when he had so clearly indicated that he was going to Miami, had to have some significance — but what was I to do about it, I couldn't think! Even Tom had seemed to have no doubt that Miami was his true destination, presumably because there were such things as the formalities he was flouting at this moment. Undoubtedly he had gone to Florida yesterday and his passport had been stamped to prove it — but he was equally undoubtedly in Haiti today.

What *was* I to do? First and foremost, I supposed, I had to keep track of him to see where he was heading. Port-au-Prince was a rabbit warren and he would be impossible to locate once he was among those teeming millions or behind the closed doors of one of those impressive villas I had admired. I raced through to the outside concourse, crowded now as the morning wore on. For a moment I thought I had already lost them, but at that second they appeared and walked swiftly through the crowd to the waiting cars outside.

Trying desperately to be both inconspicuous and casual, I managed to keep them in sight through the intervening travellers and was rewarded by the sight of a black Cadillac gilding up from nowhere and barely pausing while the two men slipped into the back seat.

A taxi-driver, standing by his decrepit car, was trying to attract my attention. Why not? I thought.

'Suivez cette voiture,' I said, pointing to the departing Cadillac and fighting down an insane desire to giggle. Could this really be happening to me?

Fortunately the taxi-driver must have been an ardent filmgoer as he seemed delighted to oblige. The Cadillac had been held up by traffic at the airport exit and we had no difficulty in keeping him in sight. No matter how powerful the car, it would have been impossible for it to reach a high speed on that road.

I delved into my bag and knotted a scarf round my hair. Hiding behind the anonymity of dark glasses, I thought it was unlikely that da Costa would recognize me, even if he happened to turn round — but he and his companion were too engrossed in conversation to be conscious of the decrepit taxi. I could see their two heads inclined together in the back seat.

We followed them through the town and along the road which I recognized as leading to Petionville. Port-au-Prince was behind and below us, and still they climbed up.

Into the square of Petionville, the gardens and the church looking as if they had been transported direct from the south of France, and ahead of us I could see the Cadillac make a right turn. The taxi stopped.

'Suivez, Suivez,' I said urgently. But it was hopeless. A nun followed by a line of children in their Sunday best was crossing the road, making for the church. We had no alternative but to stop, letting the black car disappear from sight.

After what seemed an eternity the road was clear, and the taxi turned right into the side-road taken by the Cadillac. It was a wide avenue, flanked on both sides by large houses set back from the road behind trees and high walls. There was no sign of the car.

The driver unleashed a flood of patois at me over his shoulder and came to a halt. He was obviously asking for instructions and indicating that the road led nowhere. It was a cul-de-sac, he said. What should he do?

168

Where should he go?

Where, indeed? I wished that someone would tell me, but having come so far I was not going to give up without a struggle. Asking him to wait for me, I got out of the car.

He would go to the car park, he said, indicating the square. He would wait.

I was conscious of the fact that there was no meter and price-wise I was completely at his mercy — but at that moment, that was the least of my worries. I walked down the avenue from the end nearest the square to the wall that sealed off the bottom, but although I peered down the drives to each of the impressive houses, I could see no sign of the Cadillac.

I could have wept with frustration. It seemed to me certain that da Costa must have come to pick up the heroin — the evidence so vital to the case. And here was I, within yards of him. Just a little more luck and I could have given Tom and Nick the address of the Haitian connection. I was damned if I would give up now!

Walking back again towards the square, I went a little way down the drive of the first house I came to. A white Citroen was parked outside. Not conclusive evidence, of course — the Cadillac could have been taken round the back or put in the garage, but it seemed unlikely, and I retreated, trying the house on the opposite side of the road.

I had hardly ventured more than a few paces when a small, yapping dog hurtled towards me, closely followed by his mistress who had been picking flowers in the garden.

'I'm looking for a M. Beauregard,' I said. 'Does he live here?'

She smiled and shrugged.

'No Engleesh,' she explained.

I tried it all over again in French. Not unnaturally, she had never heard of the gentleman and with many apologies I departed, but not before I had seen that there was apparently no car in the garage and none parked in front of the house.

As soon as I had turned into the drive of the house next door, I knew my search was over. Through the trees I could see the Cadillac drawn up in front of the door, but just to make completely certain, I stepped off the drive and on to the grass, through the intervening bushes. It was the car, all right — and da Costa had to be inside. Villa Maurice, it had said on the gate. Elation flooded through me.

'Qu'est-ce vous faites ici?' a harsh voice shouted behind me. I spun round. A short, squat Haitian was standing there, brandishing a machete. I think perhaps he was a gardener, but his attitude was threatening and at the time I felt certain he was about to attack me. My French deserted me utterly.

'I'm a tourist — I take pictures,' I gabbled, waving my camera. 'I'm sorry, I go now.'

'You not leave. You see master.'

He took hold of my arm and literally frog-marched me to the front door, while I continued to protest volubly every inch of the way. It was totally without avail. He rang the bell and handed me over to a forbidding looking woman with a black dress and severe, iron grey hair.

I appealed to her.

'Look,' I said. 'I'm so sorry. I didn't mean to trouble anyone. I was just taking a picture of the house — such an attractive style of architecture!'

'No Engleesh,' she said expressionlessly. 'You see Monsieur.'

I was thrust into a small room off the entrance hall and the door was locked behind me.

I gripped the edge of the gilt chair and swore at myself. So clever, I thought. So *bloody* clever — and if da Costa should see me, I'd be responsible for blowing the whole thing wide open. My only hope was to pray that he was in another room, out of sight

171

somewhere, and that the owner of the house would come alone. Then, perhaps, I might be able to bluff my way out.

I took off my scarf and dark glasses. My brief glimpse of the man at the airport had made me think that possibly he would not be entirely impervious to feminine charms. I fluffed my hair and licked my lips that had gone strangely dry. Footsteps were approaching.

He was alone as he unlocked the door and came inside. I was determined to take the initiative and took a few steps forward, my hand outstretched.

'I'm Susan Fanshawe,' I said graciously, that being the name of the school head prefect, and the first thing that came to mind. 'I'm really so terribly sorry to have caused such a fuss. I was just walking up the road and caught sight of your house — such a delightful design! I'm a student of architecture, and couldn't resist just one picture. It was unforgiveable of me not to ask permission first. Can you possibly forgive me?'

He bowed over my hand.

'Mam'selle. It is I who should apologize. My staff are a little on edge — there have been many burglaries in the district, and I have given strict instructions about intruders.

I did not anticipate such a charming one.'

His gaze flicked over me and I smiled provocatively.

'Only a Frenchman could possibly be so gallant!'

He laughed.

'As it happens, Mam'selle, I am an Italian.'

'Oh dear! Now you'll *never* forgive me! What can I do to make amends?'

'Have dinner with me, perhaps? You are staying here, in Petionville?'

'At the Hotel Fontainbleu,' I said, giving the name of George's hotel. 'I can think of nothing I'd like better than to have dinner with you. Italian men are — outside my experience.' I fluttered my eyelashes at him, knowing as I did so that I was hamming it terribly.

'That is what holidays are for, no? To enlarge the experience? Shall we say tonight, at eight?'

'I shall look forward to it. But now, you will excuse me, I'm sure. I have some concentrated shopping to do!'

I extended my hand again and once more he bowed over it, his lips actually moving over my skin. My flesh crawled, but the smile remained in place.

He escorted me to the front door and opened it. I was about to leave when I remembered that he still had not mentioned his name.

'An element of mystery is very intriguing,' I said, 'but may I know who I am to dine with tonight?'

'The name is Borelli,' he said. 'Paulo Borelli. A votre service, mam'selle.'

I hoped that this last bow had been quick enough off the mark to avoid his seeing the look of recognition which must have dawned in my eyes as he spoke the name. Borelli! Some relation, that was certain, to da Costa's playmate in Grand Guani. As we stood there making our farewells I was conscious of movement at the far end of the hall. A door was opening — someone was emerging. It could have been the housekeeper, it could have been da Costa. I did not wait long enough to find out.

With a final wave I walked briskly down the drive without looking back, realizing as I reached the road that my knees were trembling and my face felt it had been starched and ironed. Still I dared not run. I forced myself to walk normally the length of the road, but almost collapsed with relief when I saw, ahead of me, the taxi still waiting. I was not too distracted, however, to make a note of the name of the road: Paulo Borelli, Villa Maurice, Avenue des Palmiers. I had it all! Now all that remained was to transmit the information to Tom or Nick — and this is where I was so angry that I had no knowledge of their colleague in Haiti. If only I had his name and telephone number! But I didn't — and my only hope was to get on the line to Grand Guani as quickly as possible.

I thought at first of going to the Hotel Fontainbleu, which was only just round the corner; but on second thoughts I decided it would be safer not to go anywhere near it. I would phone from the airport, I thought. I looked at my watch. I was going to miss that plane, that was certain — but there were others. That was an unimportant detail. I seemed to have become an expert in missing planes over the last few days.

The taxi driver, seemingly incurious, drove me back to the airport, where he demanded (and got) a phenomenal number of dollars. I had other things on my mind.

The lines, need you ask, were engaged. There was no hope, the operator said, of getting through to Grand Guani for half an hour, at least. I waited, biting my fingernails.

Finally, after what seemed an eternity, the number was ringing. I could picture it — a cream-coloured telephone on the shelf by the door, ringing and ringing and ringing. After the first few rings I knew there was no one to answer it. Tom was not at home, and Nick must still be on his way between Haiti and Grand Guani.

I had to get word to them. Da Costa himself could be on his way with the heroin in a matter of a few minutes. The fact that Borelli was free for dinner surely meant that da Costa didn't expect to stay long. He would be back in Grand Guani within the day, with the drugs in his plane.

But they'd find it, I told myself. Didn't Tom say that all boats and planes were torn apart? No, I remembered, that wasn't what he had said. He had only specifically mentioned boats and planes from Haiti — and as far as anyone in Grand Guani knew, da Costa was flying direct from Miami. No one would expect heroin from there. All the traffic was in the opposite direction.

I *had* to let them know. On impulse I went to the flight information desk and asked the girl there if there were any flights, any flights at all, to Grand Guani.

'No,' said the girl. 'We 'ave no flights to Grand Guani.'

I switched to French, stumbling over my words in my agitation. I knew, I said that there were no — what on earth were 'scheduled flights' in French? — no flights that were in the time-table, but I was desperate! My mother was lying ill — dying perhaps — in Grand Guani, and I had no means to get to her. Was there not some other plane — some small, private plane that was flying there that day?

No, said the girl. That was strictly contrary to the regulations, to permit passengers on private planes.

I turned away, running my fingers through my hair in desperation, and sat down close to the desk while I thought out my next move. There had to be a way. I would have to try phoning again.

'Pardon, mam'selle.' A voice spoke quietly in my ear. It was an airport employee, a young, coffee-coloured boy in a smart navy-blue uniform.

'You wish to go to Grand Guani?'

'Yes, I do. Is there a plane?'

'Quiet! Follow me.' He led the way round a corner, away from the information desk. 'I could show you a plane,' he said. 'There is a man who is refuelling now. He is taking off very soon on his way to Fort Lauderdale. He would take you, I think.'

'Oh *please*,' I breathed, 'you must take me to him.'

'I take you,' he said, looking furtively over his shoulder. 'But first — you give some dollars, eh?'

I pulled out my remaining money and pushed it at him without bothering to count it.

'Wait,' I said, and pushed away to retrieve my case from the locker. I was back in an instant. 'Now take me,' I told him. 'Quickly!'

He ducked through a door marked 'Défence d'Entrer', and I followed him, down a passage and on to the tarmac. He skirted the buildings until we arrived at a bay where a neat little plane was being refuelled by two mechanics. A slim, sandy-haired freckled face young man was standing close by, wiping his hands on an oily rag. I hoped fervently that appearances were deceptive and that he was an experienced pilot, but as he cheerfully agreed to give me a lift to Grand Guani, I resolutely quelled all doubts.

'Think nothing of it,' he said when I thanked him. 'I'm glad of the company. It seemed a long haul from Jamaica with no one to talk to. I'm Joe Dexter, by the way.'

A cheerful and talkative young man, was Joe Dexter. A good deal too talkative, I thought, as we flew through the mountains that lie between Port-au-Prince and Cap Haitien. As I looked out at the towering slopes on each side of the plane, it seemed to me that we could hardly avoid brushing them with our wing-tips, but either by luck or good judgement — and I really did think it was the latter, in spite of his boyish appearance, we passed through safely and were eventually flying over the open sea.

But I did wish he would stop talking. He told me about his boss — a millionaire who had made his money out of selling hair-straightener and skin-lightener to the negroes and who had flown down to his villa in Montego Bay a few days before; and about the millionaire's son — who, by the way, was having matrimonial problems (well, his wife was an ex-Hollywood starlet, so what could you expect?) — and was borrowing the plane from tomorrow, the father having arranged to come back on a friend's yacht. And the boss's wife, now she was something else again. A real culture vulture, on a tour of the Greek islands at this moment.

My head reeled. I couldn't begin to follow the fortunes of this improbable family, but fortunately he seemed to need no comment and I was able to switch off entirely, merely nodding or raising my eyebrows from time to time. I was only thankful that this gregarious young man was flying from Jamaica to Florida on this particular day and needed to refuel in Grand Guani. For once, circumstances seemed to be on my side.

The island drew inexorably nearer. We were

flying now over the scattering of islands that were Nick's parish — West Guani, North Guani, Tree Cay and Lion Cay, as well as others that were too small to possess an airstrip or indeed to be inhabited at all.

The landing on Grand Guani took place without incident and I took my bag from Joe Dexter with heartfelt thanks. Nick's plane, I noted, had returned safely and was bedded down in its hangar.

Taxis were something that did not abound at Grand Guani airport. There were two which met the regular flight, but no one expected passengers at this hour on a Sunday afternoon. The airport was dusty and deserted.

I was about to phone the cottage once more to break the news of my arrival when I saw a car approaching in a cloud of dust. As it shrieked to a halt in front of the terminal I saw it was the new hotel car that had caused such a row between Lew and Jimmy, and that once again, in spite of Lew's strictures, Jimmy was at the wheel.

He looked astonished when he saw me waiting there.

'What the hell are you doing here? Thought we'd seen the last of you!'

'Can't keep me away,' I said, moving towards the car, my thoughts racing. What

180

possible reason could I give for such an unexpected change of plan? Jimmy himself gave me the clue.

'It's Tom Channing, isn't it? I thought there was something up at the party! Couldn't you keep away from him, Liz?'

I laughed with the air of one being found out.

'Well, you know how it is. Are you going back to the hotel, Jimmy? And if so, can I beg a lift?'

''Course. I'm just collecting a parcel of lobster tails from West Guani. Won't take a tick.'

'Sure you have Lew's permission this time?' I asked him when we were on our way back to the hotel.

'Course I have! I told you he'd get over it — he always does. He gets all steamed up, but he's forgotten all about it in no time. Seems like he has his mind on other things.'

I agreed that this could possibly be the case.

'Say, Liz,' Jimmy went on, 'What do you think about me and Minta? Do you think it would work?'

'Oh no, my boy! I'm not dishing out advice.'

'I just want your opinion, that's all.'

'In that case, I think she's a sight too good for you.'

'I know that.' Jimmy spoke humbly. 'No kidding, Liz, she's a wonderful girl — maybe the best I'm ever likely to find. You know what? Her old man's got a little store over on Back Street. Minta says that if we got married he'd retire and let us run it. There's a nice little cottage attached to it, too.'

'With roses round the door?'

'What? Oh!' he laughed, 'Well, if there aren't any, we'll plant some — or frangipani or hibiscus, or something.'

'Sounds as if you've made up your mind.'

'No, I haven't done that. But I'm thinking.'

'Life's hardly ever simple,' I said, as we drew up outside the cottage.

'No need for you to worry! Tom'll welcome you with open arms.'

'I wouldn't like to bet on it,' I said, as I opened the door and let myself out. 'Don't worry about my case. It's not heavy.'

He drove off to park the car a few yards up the road, outside the hotel but the sound of the car engine and our exchange of words had brought Tom to the cottage door and he stood transfixed as I walked up the short path towards him.

'Don't say a word,' I said. 'I'll explain it all. Where's Nick?'

182

'In the shower. He hasn't been in so long himself. They came down in West Guani for George to see someone there.'

At that point Nick appeared framed in the bedroom doorway, a towel wrapped round his waist.

'I thought I heard your voice! What the hell's all this about?'

'I tried to phone,' I said, 'but couldn't get hold of you. Then I got the chance of a lift back. Da Costa is in Haiti. He came just after you left Nick, and went to a house in the Avenue des Palmiers with a man called Paulo Borelli. I thought it must be the headquarters perhaps — the place where the heroin comes from. I followed their car and found out the address. And I *had* to let you know! I thought you might not search da Costa's plane if you didn't know he'd been in Haiti. And so I thought that if — '

'Shut up a minute,' Tom snapped. I froze.

'Start from the beginning,' he said. 'Don't miss out anything.'

I began all over again, but this time in a more orderly way. There was silence when I had finished.

Tom came over to me, his face expressionless.

'Listen here, Marshall,' he said in a tough cop's voice. 'I've had just about enough of

183

you. How many re-runs do we have to go through of Liz's Last Evening?'

I looked at him warily for a moment, not sure whether or not he was joking, but the laughter exploded from him as he hugged and kissed me.

'You did well, baby. It's good to see you back.'

'You are a wretch! You had me worried for a minute. Do you think that is the place, Tom?'

'It seems more than likely. I'll get Pierre on to it right away. Don't disappear again while I put a call through to Haiti, will you?'

Nick, who had gone to put some clothes on, came back into the room.

'Feel like a beer?' he asked.

'Do I not!' I replied, and collapsed into a chair. It felt good to be home again.

9

'It has to be there!' Tom jumped up from his chair and strode the length of the room, hands thrust deep into his pockets.

'I tell you he's clean.' Nick's voice was flat and deflated.

'They can't have looked properly.'

'They went over every inch of that plane with a fine toothcomb, Tom. You have to give Willamson credit for being thorough, if nothing else.'

We had been waiting, Tom and I, for Nick's return from the airport. Major Williamson had telephoned at eight o'clock that evening to let them know that da Costa's plane was signalled, and Nick, as the only one who had legitimate reason to be at the airport, had gone down to see what happened when the customs men got to work on the plane. The news that they had found nothing was a stunning disappointment.

'I'll bet da Costa blew his stack,' Tom said grimly.

'You're not kidding. I thought he would have an apopletic fit. But I overheard Williamson apologizing very nicely, so no doubt he'll get over it. I wouldn't be at all surprised if we get a blast from Willamson for misinforming him.'

'Oh dear, it's all my fault,' I said miserably.

'That's crazy!' Tom turned from where he had been staring unseeingly at the blank wall and came to sit near me again, taking my hand in his. 'If your information about the guy in Haiti gives us a lead, then it couldn't be more valuable. You can bet your sweet life that if da Costa wasn't there to pick up the snow, he wasn't there for a social call, either. Maybe he was making the financial arrangements.'

'And here we were thinking it would be all over bar the shouting by this time.' Nick sounded utterly weary. 'Nothing cheering from Donna's end, either. She was down at the airport meeting da Costa. She couldn't get anywhere near his study all weekend. Friend Borelli watched her like a hawk.'

'Do you think they're brothers?' I asked. 'They don't look anything like each other. The one in Haiti was a real smoothie.'

'We'll check it out, just for the record,' Tom said. 'But the important thing is where is the junk? Think, Nick. Where would you stash a couple of million dollars' worth of heroin, if you were da Costa?'

'Not in my house, that's for sure. You know

186

as well as I do it could be anywhere, Tom!'

'Is there any chance,' I put in, 'that the boat in the cave could possibly be loaded up by this time?'

'I've thought of that. It's something we ought to look into. Nick, you and I must go back down that tunnel with a camera and flashbulbs.'

'OK, boss. When?'

'Like now, man! Can you find the opening in the dark?'

'I think so.'

I listened miserably to their plans. I hated to think of them down there in the bowels of the earth, while I waited behind with my imagination working overtime.

'Can I stay here?' I asked. 'You don't want me to go back to the hotel, do you? There'd be so many explanations — besides, I must know what happens.'

'Take my bed,' Tom said. 'And don't wait up. We might be a long time.'

I watched them go, wishing there was something practical I could be doing. But at least they were able to equip themselves this time with wet suits and flasks, and other things that would make the venture incomparably easier than Nick's first trip down the tunnel.

It was a long and lonely night. Despite

Tom's instructions not to wait up, I knew it would be impossible for me to sleep and I chose a book from his varied collection on the shelves and read for as long as my eyes could take it. How long had they been away now? Three hours? My watch told me it was two o'clock, and I shivered as I thought of the two men down there in the icy water. Surely they would be back before long.

At three o'clock I went to bed and was awakened some time later by the sound of Tom and Nick returning. I struggled into my towelling robe and went to meet them, finding them exhausted and dispirited. They had searched every inch of the tunnels and caves, but had found nothing. The boat was still there and apparently devoid of drugs. Only one thing had changed — the galley was now stocked and the fuel tanks were full.

This much I learned while they were having hot showers and drinking the coffee I prepared for them. The sky was already growing lighter when Nick collapsed on to his bed and was asleep instantly. Knowing he had to fly the following day I had refused to take it, but had a tough battle with Tom who was insisting that I took his.

'I'm bushed,' he said. 'I could sleep on the floor — it doesn't matter.'

'Go on,' I ordered, giving him a push. 'For

once you'll do what I tell you.'

'One thing I sure hate,' Tom said sleepily, 'is a bossy woman!' But his eyes were already closed as I propelled him towards his bed.

The sun woke me next morning. I looked at my watch and sat up suddenly as I saw that it was already past nine o'clock, wincing as I moved my stiff shoulders. I had put the chair cushions on the floor and had managed to get a little sleep, but the make-shift mattress left much to be desired. I left it without regret. Somehow I had to rouse Nick so that he could get to work on time.

At that moment the door of the bedroom opened and Nick came into the room, pushing his shirt down inside his shorts.

'I didn't think you'd make it,' I said.

'I always make it. A built in alarm-clock, I think. Can you rustle me up some coffee, Liz?'

I did so, thinking that in this entire drama, the making of coffee seemed my major occupation.

'Tom's still dead to the world,' Nick said when he joined me again.

'Has he any jobs today? Any deadlines to meet?'

'Not that I know of.'

'I'll let him sleep, then.'

'Lucky chap.' Nick finished his coffee.

'What are you going to do?'

'Oh, I'll just be around the place. Have a swim, I expect.'

'Take care, won't you? Don't speak to any strange men.'

'Have no fear.'

I put on my bikini and went outside to the deserted beach, finding no difficulty at this hour in securing a beach chair in the shade, and stretching out, I drifted off to sleep once more.

I woke some time later to find that Jimmy had joined me, regarding me with some amusement over the lurid cover of a paper back.

'If it isn't Sleeping Beauty!' he said. 'Welcome back to the human race.'

I blinked at him.

'How long have you been here?'

'Ooh, ages!'

'Shouldn't you be working?'

He groaned.

'Do me a favour! It's me day off, isn't it? Worked all day Sunday, didn't I? Cor 'struth, surely I'm entitled to a day of rest, same as everyone else.'

'Sorry! You shouldn't have such a bad reputation.'

'Bad reputation? Innocent as a babe unborn, that's me. Not like some. Don't need to ask why you're all worn out this morning, do we?'

I leaned back and closed my eyes again.

'Go away, Jimmy, and take your nasty insinuations with you!'

'OK, Liz — you're innocent, just like me! Why don't we take our two little innocent selves out for a boat trip? Lew said I could use his this morning — that nice blue job out there.'

I raised my head from its reclining position and looked at him sceptically.

'You expect me to believe that?'

'He did, honest! I'm all in favour now, 'cos I did a lot of extra work over the weekend. Even stripped down his boat engine in me time off! So he said I could use it today. Ask him if you don't believe me.'

I subsided again, closing my eyes.

'All right, I believe you. But Araminta would have a poisoned dagger or something lethal waiting for me if I went out with you. And anyway, I'm too lazy.'

'Minta wouldn't mind,' Jimmy said. 'She knows you're sweet on Tom.'

'Then she knows more than I do,' I said tartly.

'Go on, Liz — who are you kidding?'

'The subject is not for discussion.'

'Well, come for a trip. I might not get a

191

chance like this again. Lew's what you call unpredictable.'

'Can't be bothered!'

He returned to his book with a deep sigh, but only for a few minutes.

'Lovely it is, out there,' he said, returning to the attack. 'Look how the sun sparkles on the waves. Makes you feel real poetic.'

'Go away!'

'Ever seen a flying fish, Liz? Or a turtle? Or a school of dolphins? They're all out there, you know.'

I sat up slowly and looked at him with resignation.

'How many flying fish do you guarantee?'

'No guarantees, lady!' Jimmy was already off his chair and heading towards the sea. 'I'll swim out and bring it in closer for you.'

I stood up reluctantly.

'We're not going to be long, are we Jimmy?'

'No, not long. Our towels and books will be OK — no one will take them.'

Lew's motor skiff was dwarfed by Tony da Costa's cabin cruiser that was moored beside it, but the engine roared into life at the touch of a button. Jimmy reduced it to idling speed and drifted closer to the shore, reaching out a hand to pull me aboard. Then he increased the revs again and away we went, slicing through the clear water, the wake creaming behind us.

'Great, isn't it?' Jimmy shouted above the noise of the engine.

I nodded, smiling. It was great and exhilarating and beautiful and I was glad I had come after all, in spite of all the instincts that warned me not to have anything to do with any enterprise dreamed up by the volatile Jimmy.

We saw our first flying fish after five minutes and then shoal after shoal winged out of the water in front of us to fly in an arc and dive once again into the waves.

Jimmy was delighted as if he successfully stage-managed the whole thing.

'Didn't I tell you? Maybe we'll see dolphins if we go over towards Baker's Cay.'

The island took on a new dimension seen from the sea. With spray in my face, I tried to identify various landmarks — the cottage, the road to the airport, the south point where Tom had taken me after the party.

'What place is that?' I asked, pointing to a big house on a slight knoll, surrounded by trees.

'Government House. Best beach on the island just there — I reckon the Governor has a nice easy life!'

'I expect he has his problems,' I said. 'Are we going right round the island?'

'No — it'd take too long, and there's too many coral heads. We could land on Baker's Cay, though. How about it? People say it's pretty.'

'Surely that will take too long as well?'

'Not really. Besides, we're not in that much of a hurry.'

But Tom will wake up, I thought, and I won't be there. I don't want to miss this last day.

'I don't want to be away long.'

'Relax! It's no distance.'

But it did, in fact, take longer than either of us imagined. The little island looked close, but the further we went from Grand Guani, the rougher the sea became and the slower our progress.

'Jimmy, let's go back,' I urged. 'It's getting awfully choppy.'

'It's OK — nothing to worry about,' he said stubbornly. 'We'll make it, easy.'

I subsided, as suddenly the island did look appreciably nearer, and it did look pretty and inviting, with its curve of white sand and green slopes rising from the shore. I could understand Jimmy's desire to explore it while he had the use of the boat, especially as he might not get the chance again.

I could not deny, too, that the idea of walking on a deserted beach — a beach that was washed again and again by tides that came and went without ever meeting a human footprint — had a certain fascination. I had never been on a completely uninhabited island before and the idea of it was appealing.

To give Jimmy credit, he seemed competent enough as he manœuvred us close to the shore and put down an anchor. We swam the short distance to the beach, Jimmy with his cigarettes and matches held above his head.

'Can't be without them for five minutes, can you?' I teased him. 'You smoke too much, Jimmy.'

He grinned back.

'Yes, miss. Sorry, miss.'

The green hill that rolled backwards from the beach was, we found, rather a disappointment, being covered in a tough, spiky shrub which was nothing like the grass we had hoped for. It was hard on our bare feet, but we found a path through it, almost like a sheep track except for the fact there were no sheep, and we followed it until we reached the top of the hill. Here, instead of a shallow slope to the shore, it was as if the island had been sliced by a giant machete, so that the cliffs were sheer, and the sea — so calm and friendly where we had landed — was shadowed and rough.

We sat for a while, Jimmy smoking a

cigarette, as we watched the waves crashing on the rocks beneath them.

'It's almost like Cornwall,' I said.

'I went to St Ives once,' Jimmy remarked.

'Did you like it?'

'It rained every day and I had mumps.'

'Not a fair test!'

'No, I s'pose not.' He settled back more comfortably on one elbow. 'It's nice here though, isn't it? I mean, in the sunshine. I reckon I could stay here and be happy.'

'Do you, Jimmy? Honestly? You wouldn't get restless after a few months or a few years and want to push off again, footloose and fancy free?'

'I know what you're trying to say,' he said, suddenly serious. 'It's hard to know, isn't it? I have this feeling that if I pass up the chance of Minta and the store and the cottage, I would regret it for the rest of me life. OK, so sometimes I'm going to feel trapped — well, what's new? I've always felt trapped! But somehow, I feel that by staying here, I'd feel less trapped than I ever have before. Everything I enjoy is here — this kind of free and easy life, I mean. Walking around without shoes, and fishing, and sitting on the beach at night, playing me guitar. And Minta, of course. She's a marvellous girl, Liz.'

'That's quite a speech,' I said.

'Yeah, well . . . I really mean it. I love that girl. I think we can make it.'

'Then go ahead and make it. It's up to you.' I laughed a little. 'Is it something about these islands, Jimmy? All this falling in love?'

'So you are sweet on Tom?'

I shook my head.

'Honestly, Jimmy, I don't know. I've known him for less than a week and disliked him for part of that. Sometimes I think the island has cast a spell on me.'

'He'd suit you, I reckon. I mean, you'd need a tough character. You'd give someone like me a dog's life! But Tom's pretty bright, and tough as hell. Can't think why he's wasting his time being a diver down here.'

'Perhaps he's like you he just likes the life.'

Talking of Tom had made me want to get back, and I got to my feet.

'He'll be wondering where I am,' I said. 'Can we go now, Jimmy?'

'Any time!'

We followed a path which led steeply down to the far end of the curving beach on which we had landed and walked along the sand, self-important sandpipers strutting away in front of us. A large, half-buried conch shell caught my eye and I stopped to dig it out, while Jimmy walked on.

'This is gorgeous,' I said. 'Just look at the

lovely, pearly pink inside of it, Jimmy.'

But Jimmy wasn't listening. I heard him give a shout — a sort of strangled cry, and looked up to see him staring straight ahead.

'What's wrong?' I shouted. He pointed further along the beach and shouted something incomprehensible over his shoulder. I started to run, my feet sinking into the soft sand, not knowing what to expect. My vision was still limited by the curve of the beach and I had no idea what Jimmy had seen to cause such consternation.

But as I joined him and followed the direction of his pointing finger I was left in no doubt. The boat had gone.

10

We both stumbled over the soft sand, Jimmy racing me to the point where we had come ashore. He stood looking out to sea, his hand shading his eyes as he stared out towards the horizon. Wordlessly he turned and pointed out to sea as I joined him at the water's edge. The boat was tossing up and down in the waves, almost out of sight and drifting steadily further and further away from us in the direction of West Guani.

A sudden rage shook me.

'Oh *Jimmy!*' I stormed, 'how could you be so stupid! You can't have anchored it properly! Now what on earth are we going to do?'

'I thought it was OK.' Any trace of his usual high spirits was effectively erased. 'I s'pose I didn't realize what a swell there was. It seems to have got rougher.'

I turned my back on him and walked a few paces away, not trusting myself to speak. It was all so typical! I should have followed that instinct that told me to have nothing to do with Jimmy's exploits. Something always seemed to go wrong — but never before quite so disastrously wrong as this.

He came up to me, his face the picture of woe.

'I'm sorry, Liz,' he said. 'Honest, I wouldn't have had it happen for the world. What the hell is Lew going to say?'

Angry as I was, I realized that no purpose would be served by continuing to rant at Jimmy, who had certainly bought himself a peck of trouble by his carelessness. Anyway, it was partly my own fault for relying on him to make sure the boat was fast. No one knew better than I that in some ways he was irresponsible as a child.

'So now what do we do?' I asked, forcing myself to speak calmly. 'Attract the attention of a passing boat? Only there don't seem to be any.'

'We're in the flight path to West Guani,' Jimmy said. 'Maybe we could wave something when the plane goes over.'

'What do you suggest?'

We looked at each other, and in spite of the seriousness of our situation, we burst out laughing. Jimmy was clad in gaudy but brief swimming trunks, while I was wearing a pink checked cotton bikini. Neither of us had what one might regard as any surplus clothing about our persons.

Which reminded me that I was beginning

to feel the first glow of sunburn — a problem that was obviously going to get a lot more acute if we were to be marooned on that treeless island for long.

'We're going to need shade, Jimmy.'

'We're going to need a lot of things we haven't got; but at least I've got me fags and matches. We'd better make a fire on that highest point. Someone might notice.'

'Good idea,' I agreed. 'There's quite a lot of driftwood over there. We'd better start moving it.'

By the time we had been up and down that track half a dozen times pulling pieces of wood and anything else inflammable we could find, I was not quite so sure that it was such a good idea. My hair was soaked with sweat and plastered to my head. Perspiration rolled down my face and into my eyes, heads down, we toiled up that hill time after time. My shoulders and thighs, now a bright pink, were beginning to burn intolerably.

I tried not to think about my need for a drink.

While Jimmy started the fire I went down the hill again, and this time immersed myself in the sea, luxuriating in the comparative coolness of the water. For a while I floated mindlessly, until the hum of a distant aircraft penetrated my consciousness. It was Nick on his homeward trip from West Guani.

I rushed out of the water waving wildly as he flew high overhead. The fire was beginning to burn. I could see a thin wisp of smoke, but no flames were visible in the glaring sunshine. Would Nick or anyone else in the plane notice that anything was amiss — or even if they saw the fire, would they think we were enjoying a pleasant barbecue? Illogically I shouted; but implacably the plane flew on, back to Grand Guani. No one had noticed that we were stranded on this inhospitable rock.

There were still no boats to be seen, though I scanned the horizon, willing someone to appear. In spite of the waters that teemed with fish, there were few full-time fishermen on the island. For most it was a leisure-time occupation and the Monday morning sea was empty.

I trailed dejectedly back to Jimmy.

'I don't think this fire business is going to work after all,' he said. 'Not until someone actually comes looking for us. Maybe we should save the wood until it gets dark, otherwise we might find we run out when we most need it.'

'When it gets *dark*!' I must have sounded horrified. Darkness was hours away — surely someone would find us before then.

'Well, when do you reckon we'll be missed?'

'I've no idea,' I said, thinking it over. 'Nick's going straight out on another flight, so won't know I'm not around. Tom will wonder where I am, I expect, but I imagine he'll just think I've gone off somewhere on my own. I don't know when it'll dawn on him that there's something wrong.'

'No one will miss me, that's for sure. Minta's working until late this evening, so I'm not seeing her until tomorrow, and Lew pushed off somewhere quite early. He said he was going to be busy, so I don't suppose he'll even notice the boat's gone.' He sat down, his back against an outcrop of rock. 'Have a fag?'

'Thanks, I will. Maybe it'll take my mind off my thirst.'

'Don't remind me! There's a couple of cans of beer in the locker of the boat.'

'Shut up, Jimmy, I can't bear it!'

'Hey!' he said, noticing my sunburn for the first time. 'That'll give you hell soon.'

'It already is, but what can I do? There's no shade anywhere. To think I thought this island was pretty! It's the most horrible barren rock I've ever seen — no water, no shade, no nothing.'

'That looks like a cave down there,' Jimmy said, indicating the sheer cliff with his cigarette. 'I wonder if you could get down to it.'

I got up and looked down towards the shadowed cleft about two thirds of the way down towards the sea.

'Fine for a mountain goat,' I said. 'I'd never make it.' But the idea fascinated me nevertheless. If there was one cave, I thought, perhaps there were others, particularly if the geological formation was the same as Grand Guani, and maybe not all were in such an inaccessible position. I wandered off to explore.

A grazed knee and two broken fingernails later I decided that although there were small fissures in the rocks, there was nowhere else that looked big enough to accomodate me. It seemed that I would just have to put up with those merciless rays, and I went back to where Jimmy had now banked down the fire, preserving our stock of driftwood for later.

He looked at me, concerned and worried.

'There must be some way we can make a shelter,' he said.

'I can't see how, Jimmy. Don't worry about it! I'll survive.'

He looked down at the cave again.

'If only you could get down there! It wouldn't be impossible, you know. If you climbed down a bit further along — over there, where the cliff isn't so steep — you could swim to just below the cave and hoist yourself up on the ledge.'

I considered the proposition doubtfully.

'It's awfully rough,' I said. 'And even if I could swim over to the cave, I don't know whether I could hoist myself up there. I'm not one of nature's athlete's!'

'I could help you. We might be hours yet! Honest, Liz, you could really do yourself a mischief.'

'What about you?'

'Oh, my hide's like leather! I'll come back here and hang about in case anyone shows up. Come on, Liz — let's give it a go. We won't be worse off if you can't make it.'

'That's true,' I agreed.

But I still felt doubtful as we clambered down the cliff that grew steadily rockier and more perilous as we descended. I hesitated on the brink, looking despairingly at the cave and the waves crashing against the cliff below it.

'Jimmy, I *can't*,' I wailed.

'Come on, I've got you!'

The swim across was comparatively easy, but pulling myself up was even worse than I had anticipated. Time after time I failed, being sucked down by the waves, but at last Jimmy managed to haul himself on to the ledge, and bracing himself against the cliff and holding on to the twisted root of one of the stunted bushes that was all the vegetation this island produced, he managed to pull me up beside him.

For a moment we stood there panting, too winded to speak. Jimmy recovered first.

'We'll worry about getting you back when it arises,' he said, peering into the cave. 'You'll be nice and snug in there — it's well above the water line. Go on, get yourself under cover.'

Perversely, now that I was within inches of the shade I had desired so much, I felt reluctant to isolate myself from Jimmy.

'Couldn't you stay?' I asked.

'Better not. We don't want to miss anyone, do we? I'll give you a shout from time to time.'

I raised no more arguments and went inside the cave opening. It was wide and shallow at first, but tapered off at the back. The floor was hard and rocky, and I tentatively sat down, keeping a wary eye open for crabs or lizards.

Jimmy looked in through the opening.

'OK?' he asked.

'Just fine,' I assured him. 'Take care of yourself. Keep in touch.'

It was blissfully cool and dark in the cave,

and I leaned back against the unyielding rock, trying desperately to keep my mind off my burning thirst.

'Think of the good things,' I told myself. Like Nick, and the fact that we're friends again. And Tom? Was he a good thing? I was desperately afraid of assuming too much, but it was an undeniable fact that the thought of him was comforting and familiar. I knew he would feel hurt when he discovered that I had gone off somewhere on my last day, apparently ignoring him. How long before his hurt turned to concern?

A furry body swooped from the darkness at the back of the cave into the brightness, and as swiftly back again, missing me by a whisker. I cringed back against the rock, shuddering. What a fool I was about creepy-crawlies! I forced myself to relax. I might have known that I could expect to find bats in caves, and reason told me there was nothing to fear. All those stories about bats being tangled in people's hair was nothing but fiction, I knew — but even so, I hoped he and his friends and relations would stay back there in the dark, well out of sight. I knew that if many of the furry creatures started swooping around in that confined space, no power on earth would keep me there. I would be forced to take my chance with the burning sun outside.

I looked at my watch. Still only just after one o'clock. Nick would probably be snatching a sandwich before his afternoon flight, while Tom was perhaps wondering for the first time why I had not put in an appearance at the cottage.

There was nothing I could do about the situation. Jimmy would do all he could if the plane passed over-head again, I knew, but I had little hope that anyone would begin to look for us seriously for some time yet. There was no help for it but to pass the time as calmly as possible.

Why didn't I ever take more interest in geology? I looked about me at the rock formation of my refuge, and was ashamed that I had no idea what substance it consisted of, or if this type of cave system was common in the West Indies. I resolved to look it up the minute I was within reach of the good old Encyclopædia Brittanica again. All I knew was that it was grey and hard, and not at all comfortable against my sore back. There seemed, too, to be a vein of white, shining substance at the back of the cave, just below the aperture where the bat had disappeared. I had no intention of risking a futher encounter with the creature by investigating it.

Unbelievably, I was now beginning to feel

cold. I ducked out of the cave and on to the ledge from where I could see Jimmy sitting motionless and rather forlorn by the pile of driftwood. He looked as if he were singing to himself.

I shouted to him and waved, and he waved back.

'Everything OK?' he called.

'Fine!' I shouted back.

The heat outside was almost tangible and I retreated thankfully into the cool darkness of the cave where once again I tried to make myself comfortable against the rock. This time I succeeded so well that I even drifted off into a kind of half-sleep, waking eventually to find my craving for water almost intolerable.

My spirits were at their lowest ebb yet. It had been a mistake to sleep. Waking to the reality of the cave and our unchanged position was depressing to say the least.

I went out and exchanged another shout with Jimmy. He'd been asleep, too, and looked about as cheerful as I felt, though as soon as he saw me on the ledge he straightened up and tried to look alert and hopeful.

Coming back inside again, my eye fell on that white vein of rock, faintly luminous in the gloom. It made me think of glaciers and snow and ice, which in turn reminded me of long, cold, frosted glasses of iced water.

I forced my mind away from such unprofitable thoughts. Funny about that white strata, I thought, so different from the rest of the rock. Maybe I've discovered gold!

If it weren't for the bats, I said to myself, I'd go up and look at it more closely, and hard on the heels of that thought came amused derision at this ridiculous phobia of mine. Look at you, woman, I said to myself — one hundred and twenty pounds of solid flesh, scared out of your wits by a little thing no longer than your finger! Pull yourself together and go and have a look!

Gingerly I groped my way to the back of the cave. The bats kept themselves to themselves, much to my relief, but I found myself growing more puzzled by the white vein of rock, just above the level of my head, the closer I approached it. It was of such a different appearance and texture from the rest of the rock beneath it. Above it the rock was a uniform grey. Nerving myself, and hoping against hope that my hand would not come into contact with a small, furry body, I reached up to touch the shiny surface of the rock.

It was soft and yielding, and to my amazement, part of it came away in my hand, just as if I were reaching for a bag of sugar from a shelf in a supermarket. Unbelievingly, I stared at what I was holding in my hand, and looked back again to the rock shelf where I could now see bag upon bag neatly stacked from one side to the other.

It had to be the cache that Tom and Nick had been searching for. It had to be the heroin.

There was a shout from outside the cave.

'Anyone home? Hey, Liz — are you OK?'

Still holding the polythene packet, I went out to the mouth of the cave. Jimmy was in the process of hauling himself up to the ledge and was too engrossed to notice it, but his eyes fell on it the moment he had steadied himself.

'What've you got there?'

'Something I've found inside. There's a whole stack of it, Jimmy.'

'Let's have a look.' He held out his hand and I passed the packet over, feeling even as I did so that I was wrong. I should have kept my discovery to myself, but he had caught me on the hop, before I'd adjusted myself to the idea. He looked at it closely, and when he spoke, his voice was hoarse with excitement.

'You know what this is, don't you?'

'I think I can guess!'

'What else can it be but dope? Snow, I should think.'

He broke open the packet, ignoring my protests, took some powder on the end of his finger and licked it cautiously.

'That's what it is, all right. You say there's a lot more inside? It must be worth millions! Let's go and look.'

He dived into the cave and I followed.

'It's all right at the back,' I said. 'Up high, on that ledge.'

He turned back to me, looking as if he had been hit with a sledge-hammer.

'That little lot would be worth a fortune,' he said, awe in his voice. 'Millions! I s'pose you wouldn't consider keeping quiet about it and splitting the proceeds?'

I looked at him.

'You're joking, of course!'

He laughed, rather shamefaced.

'Yeah, I guess I am. Set us up for life though, wouldn't it?' He sighed regretfully. 'Some bastard stands to make a mint.'

'Spread a load of misery, you mean — not to mention the chance of years in jail.'

'Guess you're right. Have you ever tried it, Liz?'

'Never. Have you?'

'Well, not this stuff — I wouldn't touch heroin with a barge pole, but I've had the odd

212

joint. Don't go for it a lot.'

'I'm glad to hear it,' I said.

But Jimmy was not interested in my comments and was still staring, thunderstruck, at the packet.

'How do you suppose it got there, Liz?'

I was silent for a moment. I was wondering if I should tell him the whole story and win his co-operation but decided against it even as the thought occurred to me, in view of his proven unreliability. If Tom or Nick wanted to explain to him, that was up to them; my part, I felt, was to play it cool and give nothing away.

'Heaven knows,' I said. 'I suppose it must have been smuggled.'

It all fits, I was thinking. A rendezvous at sea, Tom had said. No doubt an innocent-looking Haitian sloop of the kind that brought fruit and vegetables to Grand Guani several days a week had landed the heroin in the cave before going on to the main island and submitting to the search by Customs. And even now, Tony da Costa's secret cabin cruiser was fuelled and ready to come and pick it up. No one could possibly have expected it to be found. There were, it is true, occasional picnickers on the island at weekends, but as we had proved all too conclusively, the island and its surrounding waters were utterly deserted during the week. And only sheer desperation had persuaded me to climb down to the cave. It was hard to imagine that a casual visitor would have bothered.

But nevertheless, they must have decided to take a calculated risk in leaving the goods there, and to me it seemed to point to one thing. Da Costa would never risk leaving it for long. In other words, it could be a toss-up whether da Costa or our rescuers made the island first.

'We'd better leave it here,' I said.

'No choice. We'd never be able to carry it back — which reminds me, Liz, that's what I came for. To tell you that you'll never make it if you don't come now. I think the wind's changed, the sea's come up something chronic. If it gets any rougher, we'll have had it.'

I went out on the ledge again and looked at the sea. My heart sank. It had been rough enough when we made the journey over, but now the waves were crashing against the rocks, sending spray yards up into the air.

'Oh, *dear*,' I said, inadequately. 'Oh, Jimmy!'

'We've got to try,' he said. 'It's not going to get any better. Look, I'll go in first, and you sort of lower yourself and hang on to me.'

We followed this programme which sounded a lot easier in theory than it proved in practice. The swell forced me away from the point on the cliff we were making for, and without doubt I would have been swept under the waves completely if Jimmy hadn't supported me valiantly. But after a frightening ten minutes or so, which I trust never to be forced to repeat in the whole of my life, we managed to make the rocks, being flung upon them with such force that we both skinned our legs and hands.

For a moment we lay there, panting, but finally summoned the energy to climb the path to the pile of driftwood.

'I think we'd better light it now,' Jimmy said. 'They must be looking for us by this time.'

I subsided full length on the spiky ground, an arm flung across my eyes. Jimmy came and squatted down beside me.

'You're OK, aren't you? Maybe that cave wasn't such a good idea after all.'

'I'm all right, honestly,' I said. 'And they must start looking soon. Tom will come and find us.'

'In this sea? Don't make me laugh!'

I sat up and looked at him.

'What do you mean? Of course he'll come.'

'Not in his boat, he won't.'

'Who's, then?'

'Tony da Costa's, I should think. It's the handiest. I think the Police launch went over to Lion Cay this morning.'

'But why should da Costa come for us?'

'You don't know about island life, do you? Everyone helps at a time like this. You don't know when you're going to need help yourself.'

I stared at him in silence for a moment, trying to adjust myself to the idea of being rescued by Tony da Costa, and shook my head in disbelief. Jimmy was right — this island life was outside my normal experience.

I lay down again, too tired and dispirited to think straight. I felt I had been on that island for at least a month and was fit for nothing but a sort of mindless acceptance of the situation and a longing for the moment when I could dump everything into the combined laps of Tom and Nick.

So we waited, and in a while, when the sun had all but disappeared below the horizon, I sat up and hugged myself.

'It's cold!' I said, with surprise.

'Bound to be,' Jimmy said philosophically. 'Getting hot and burnt like we did, we're bound to feel it.' He slapped at his upper arm. 'The mosquitoes have started, too.'

It was just one more misery to add to the

216

countless miseries of that day. As the darkness increased, so did the whining of the insects around us. I slapped at them ineffectually. However many I disturbed from feeding on my exposed body, there were always more to take their place. My face was throbbing and my lips swollen, and the cold bit deeper into me by the moment.

The fire was a beacon that must have been seen a long way off.

'It's so damn' rough now, it's going to take them a time to get here,' Jimmy said, but even as he spoke he pointed out to sea. 'Look,' he shouted. 'There are some lights. Liz, someone's coming.'

I jumped to my feet and strained my eyes into the darkness. Sure enough there were two lights, dipping up and down as a boat neared the island.

'Let's go down to the beach,' Jimmy said, grabbing a lighted piece of wood to illumine the way.

It seemed at that point that the warmth and security of home were only minutes away, and I was ill-prepared for the difficulty that we would have in boarding the cabin cruiser that was now approaching. Jimmy's guess had been right. The boat that had come to rescue us was the one belonging to Tony da Costa — the one we had passed so gaily that morning when we set out for our trip.

She was not having an easy passage. Time and time again the boat seemed to come nearer, only to retreat again.

'It's the coral heads,' Jimmy said. 'You can't see them at night. They need more light.'

As if in reply to his words, a bright spotlight sliced through the darkness and by the light of it, slowly and warily, at times almost disappearing from view in the tossing waves, the boat neared the shore. At last I could hear a voice — Tom's voice, as he shouted out of the darkness.

'Liz — hi, Liz! Are you OK?'

I tried to shout back, but my dry throat would emit no more than a croak and I had to content myself with waving wildly. As they came in close, I could see two figures leaning over the bows, to port and starboard, guiding the man at the helm past the murderous coral heads. Thank God — both Nick and Tom were on board. I felt at that moment I couldn't care less if the boat were piloted by the devil himself.

The next few minutes were to remain a blur. When I thought about it afterwards, I could see both Tom and Nick leaping into the waves and hanging on to the bows like grim death as they attempted to keep the craft steady and prevent it from swinging round.

'As near as we can come,' I heard Nick shout, the wind taking away some of his words.

'Come on then, Liz,' Jimmy said, but I was already running into the heavy sea, coming to a sudden halt as the full force of the waves hit me. Jimmy caught me and held me up, shouting incomprehensible words in my ear, but somehow managing to propel me forward until I could reach Tom's outstretched hand. The sides of the boat reared up frighteningly in front of me, but Tom was there to hold me and somehow he and Jimmy managed to get my feet on the ladder where for a moment I clung, incapable of further movement.

'Hold on,' came a voice above me. I looked up to see Tony da Costa reaching down to me, and thankfully I grasped his hand and found myself on the tossing deck at last. Borelli, I noticed, was at the wheel.

A blanket was produced from somewhere and put around my shoulders and da Costa urged me to go and sit in the cabin, but I shook him off. I wasn't going to leave the deck until I saw that both Nick and Tom — and of course, Jimmy — were safely on board.

Jimmy was the first to appear, then Nick, and lastly Tom, who had been hanging on to the starboard bow, keeping it steady for the others. He collapsed on to the deck for a moment, winded, but sat up at last, shaking his dripping hair out of his eyes. We looked at each other across the length of the deck, and he smiled weakly.

'Hi,' he said.

Now I could relax. Now I could go to the cabin. All explanations could come later. The important thing was that we were all safe, and as I looked at Tom, I had a sudden feeling that I had indeed been rescued, in more ways than one.

Somebody tried to make me drink some brandy, but after the first spluttering gasp I pushed it away and asked for water. Even that was difficult to get down at first, but gradually my throat eased, and I raised a laugh by asking for the brandy again, only to find that Jimmy had drunk both his glass and mine, so that another had to be produced.

I began to feel some return to normality as warmth flooded back. Tom and Nick seemed on incredibly good terms with da Costa. Had the whole thing been a mistake, I wondered? But I answered myself immediately: nothing had changed. They always *had* been on good terms with him.

Jimmy, shrouded in another blanket was sipping yet another brandy opposite me in the small cabin. Nick was sitting next to him and Tom was next to me, listening to Jimmy's shame-faced account of how we came to be marooned on the island, and da Costa was standing in the hatchway between the cabin and the open deck, smiling in a superior sort of way that revealed his contempt for such inefficient behaviour.

'The heat must have been sheer hell,' Nick said.

'It was,' I replied, trying at the same time to catch Jimmy's eye and prevent him telling about our find in the cave. Why, oh why, hadn't I trusted him with at least a censored explanation? I could see the words trembling on his lips, even before he was aware of them himself.

He swallowed his drink convulsively as he tried to get the words out.

'The cave, Liz. We forgot to tell them about the cave.'

'Oh, it was nothing,' I said repressively, hoping he would take the hint.

'Nothing! You call all that heroin nothing?'

There was a small but charged silence.

'Heroin?' I said foolishly, forcing myself not to look at da Costa.

'For God's sake, Liz, have you gone barmy? There was all this snow, Nick — packets of it. You believe me, don't you, Tom?'

'Sure,' Tom said, briefly and expression-lessly.

'*Oh*-kay,' said da Costa from the hatchway. At last I allowed myself to turn and look at him and somehow it seemed only to be expected that a small, snub-nosed gun had appeared in his hand. He was still smiling, but his eyes were cold.

'So now we know,' he said. 'It occurred to me to wonder whether you'd find it, all those hours you spent on that little island. I'm sorry.'

'You should be,' Tom said. 'Your friend in Haiti is in jail right now — I guess it won't be long before he sings. You can't win this one, da Costa. Turn yourself in.'

'With four million bucks stashed in that cave? No chance.'

'Be your age, da Costa. We know where it comes from, where it's refined, where it goes to, where it is right now. You can't win.'

'No? Only you people know where it is right now. Get rid of you and I'm riding high. All I have to do is sell it and disappear some place. OK, so I can't use the Haitian connection again, but that's the way it goes. You win some, you lose some. This happens to be the one you're all going to lose.'

'All of us swept overboard, huh?'

'Tom, I couldn't have put it better myself.'

Jimmy had been listening to this exchange with an expression of utter incredulity on his face, a cigarette suspended halfway to his lips. He dropped it and swore as it burnt his fingers. Da Costa jerked the gun in his direction.

'Don't make any sudden moves, son. Easy does it.'

Jimmy froze, licking his lips nervously.

'Stop the engine while we're going over the edge of the deep,' da Costa called over his shoulder to Borelli.

Nick and Tom exchanged a look. I knew they were thinking of the sharks and barracuda that abounded there. If and when our bodies were found, da Costa could be sure there would be no evidence of gunshot wounds.

'It's a heavy sea,' da Costa said conversationally. 'Too bad these rescue attempts sometimes end so tragically. You just got swept away in that swell near Baker's Cay. Everyone's going to be so sorry — at least, I guess some will. To others it'll be a welcome break in routine. Something to talk about. Life gets kind of dull on an island like Grand Guani.'

He smiled at us, enjoying the situation.

When would he shoot? Would he wait until we were right over the deep, or would he kill us first so that we could be tossed overboard with the minimum of delay? Suddenly it seemed very important to hang on to every second of this precious life.

I looked at Tom. I guessed that his mind was working furiously and knew that he was assessing the distance between himself and da Costa, weighing up the possibility of jumping him. Da Costa reached out and pulled me roughly to my feet, my blanket slipping off as he did so.

'Get over there,' he ordered, pushing me towards the bows so that I staggered and almost fell. He was now directly facing me from his vantage point just forward of the hatchway.

'Don't get any ideas,' he said, covering me with the gun. 'One move from you and she'll get it.'

The cruiser slowed down. We must be nearing the deep, I thought. Finally the engine died altogether and the slap-slap of the waves against the sides of the boat was the only noise to be heard. I realized that I was trembling convulsively. The end could be only seconds away.

'Drop that gun, da Costa. I have you covered,' came an authoritative, upper-class English voice that brooked no argument, from some point just beyond his left shoulder. Major Williamson's voice. A look of astonishment came over da Costa's face and for a moment his attention wavered.

Only for a moment, but it was enough for Tom, who in one swift movement picked up my discarded blanket from the deck and hurled it in da Costa's face. Immediately both Tom and Nick were on him, wresting the gun from his grasp. Forestalling any shouts for help, Tom gave him an uppercut which sent him crashing to the floor of the cabin.

Borelli came blundering through the hatchway, alarmed by the noise. He stopped transfixed as he saw Tom standing there, the gun trained on him unwaveringly.

'Just hold it right there, Borelli,' Tom said. 'Nick, take the wheel. Jimmy, get some rope — you'll find some in that outside locker. Bring it here, will you? Now, take this and keep them covered while I put them out of action.'

Jimmy, enjoying himself hugely, sat with the gun trained on the two men, while Tom. swiftly and effectively, roped them together, back to back.

'I don't get it,' I said faintly, having collapsed on the seat beside Jimmy, still shaking like a leaf. 'Where did the Major come from? Where is he now?'

'That was me, love,' Jimmy said, with an

enormous grin. 'The old master of mime and mimicry, remember?'

'You have hidden talents,' Tom said dryly, taking the gun from him now that Borelli and da Costa were immobilized, but continuing to keep it trained on them. 'Brains you haven't even used yet.'

'I say, old boy,' said Jimmy, back in his Major Williamson role as a stream of invective came from da Costa on the floor. 'That's a bit strong, what? Ladies present, don't you know?'

The action suggested by da Costa made it clear that he, for one, was not amused.

★ ★ ★

'All ready?' Nick asked.

It was almost two o'clock, but I had not long been awake from a deep, sedated sleep.

'I think so,' I said foggily, looking round the room to see if I had left anything. 'Oh — the picture, Nick! Could you bear to part with it? I'd love to have it, if you wouldn't mind.'

'You're more than welcome,' Nick said, taking it down from the wall. 'But do you really need a souvenir of the island? I shouldn't imagine you'll ever forget it.'

'I won't. For lots of reasons. Nick, where's Tom?'

'Tying up a few loose ends with Major Williamson. They're arranging for Lew and Borelli and da Costa to be extradited — I imagine we'll be escorting them when we leave on Thursday's plane. But he'll be at the airport to see you off.'

'How's Betty?'

'Pretty shattered, poor woman, though she must have had some sort of clue what was going on. Jimmy and Araminta are running the hotel — would you believe?'

'There's a lot of good in that young man,' I said. 'He's what you might call a late developer.'

'You'll be late if we don't get down to the airport!'

'Hang on — I've got to fit this picture in the top of my case.'

I finally managed to shut it and lock it, and giving a last look round the room, gathered up my hand baggage and followed Nick to the car.

There was little time to spare. My luggage was checked through immediately, but I could only give scant attention to the forms that, once again, I was required to complete. Any moment I would be called to the aircraft, and there was still no sign of Tom.

'Will passengers for Miami and Fort Lauderdale please board the aircraft?'

I looked round wildly. A car was approaching the aircraft in a cloud of dust and skidded to a halt outside. Tom leapt from it and came striding over to me.

Now that he was there, no words would come. We looked at each other, not speaking, not touching.

I was aware of Nick's voice in the background.

'Tell Dad I'll be home soon. Tell him I'm probably getting some promotion, and give him my love.'

'This is the last call for passengers to Miami and Fort Lauderdale,' came the voice again. 'Please take leave of your friends and proceed to the aircraft.'

'Goodbye, Nick,' I said to my brother. He bent and kissed me.

I turned to Tom. He put his hand out and touched my cheek.

'See you, honey,' he said gently.

'You'd better believe it,' I told him.

We do hope that you have enjoyed reading this large print book.

Did you know that all of our titles are available for purchase?

We publish a wide range of high quality large print books including:
Romances, Mysteries, Classics
General Fiction
Non Fiction and Westerns

Special interest titles available in large print are:
The Little Oxford Dictionary
Music Book
Song Book
Hymn Book
Service Book

Also available from us courtesy of Oxford University Press:
Young Readers' Dictionary
(large print edition)
Young Readers' Thesaurus
(large print edition)

For further information or a free brochure, please contact us at:
Ulverscroft Large Print Books Ltd.,
The Green, Bradgate Road, Anstey,
Leicester, LE7 7FU, England.
Tel: (00 44) **0116 236 4325**
Fax: (00 44) **0116 234 0205**

Antique dealing has its own equivalent to 'insider trading', as Charles Ramsay finds out to his cost. Offered the purchase of a lifetime, he sees all his ambitions realised in an antique jade cup, known as the 'Loot'. But as soon as the deal is irrevocably struck he finds himself stuck with it like an albatross around his neck — unable to export it without a licence, unable to sell it at home, and in a paralysing no man's land where nobody has sufficient capital to take it off his hands . . .

NO TIME LIKE THE PRESENT

June Barraclough

Daphne Berridge, who has never married, has retired to the small Yorkshire village of Heckcliff where she grew up, intending to write the biography of an eighteenth-century woman poet. Two younger women are interested in her project: Cressida, Daphne's niece, who lives in London, and is uncertain about the direction of her life; and Judith, who keeps a shop in Heckcliff, and is a divorcee. When an old friend of Daphne falls in love with Judith, the question — as for Cressida — is marriage or independence. Then Daphne also receives a surprise proposal.

SEARCH FOR A SHADOW

Kay Christopher

On the last day of her holiday Rosemary Roberts met an intriguing American in the foyer of her London hotel. By some extraordinary coincidence, Larry Madison-Jones was due to visit the tiny Welsh village where Rosemary lived. But how much of a coincidence was Larry's erratic presence there? The moment Rosemary returned home, her life took on a subtle, though sinister edge — Larry had a secret he was not willing to share. As Rosemary was drawn deeper into a web of mysterious and suspicious occurrences, she found herself wondering if Larry really loved her — or was trying to drive her mad . . .

THREE WISHES

Barbara Delinsky

Slipping and sliding in the snow as she walks home from the restaurant where she's worked for fourteen years, Bree Miller barely has time to notice the out-of-control lorry, headed straight for her. All Bree remembers of that fateful night is a bright light, and a voice granting her three wishes. Are they real or imagined? And who is the man standing over her bedside when finally she wakes up? Soon Bree finds herself the recipient of precisely those things she'd most wanted in life — even that which had seemed beyond all reasonable hope.

WEB OF WAR

Hilary Grenville

Claire Grant, a radar operator in the WAAF, still mourning the death of her parents and brother in an air raid, finds coming on leave to her grandmother's home difficult to face. Martin, a friend from her school days, now a pilot in the RAF, helps her to come to terms with her grief and encourages the flimsy rapport between Claire and her grandmother. War rules their lives and it is some time before they meet again. Claire is in love, but there are many quirks of fate yet to be faced.